365 MONKEY TRICKS

© 1995 Rebo Productions, Lisse
© 1997 Published by Rebo Productions Ltd
Text: *Maike Karstkarel*
Illustrations: *Maan Jansen*
Production: *TextCase, The Netherlands*
Translation: *Francesca Kudryashova*
for First Edition Translations Ltd, Great Britain
Typesetting: *Cardinal Graphics*
for First Edition Translations Ltd, Great Britain

ISBN 1 901094 25 1

365
MONKEY TRICKS
bedtime stories

illustrator: Maan Jansen
author: Maike Karstkarel

REBO
PRODUCTIONS

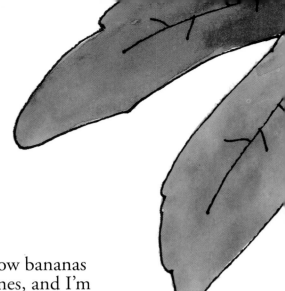

1 January

A flying banana?

"Look up there," says Micky Monkey. "See those yellow bananas at the top of the tree? Those are the really delicious ones, and I'm going to pick them!" "That's far too high," says his sister Millie. "There isn't anything to hold onto. You're bound to fall!"

"Oh no, not me," replies Micky, "I'm very good at climbing." He climbs up the trunk of the tree. Millie watches him climb higher and higher, until he is almost as high as the bananas. Golly, that's very high, she thinks.

"Look at me!" cries out Micky as he pulls at a banana. But the banana doesn't want to let go. Micky tugs hard at the stubborn banana. This time it does break off, but Micky has to grab the tree quickly to stop himself falling. The banana falls down to the ground, and lands right in Millie's arms.

Thank you very much, thinks Millie. She takes the skin off the banana and quickly eats it up. "Mmm, I enjoyed that," she says, and throws the banana skin away.

Micky has climbed down the tree and notices the banana skin lying on the ground. He looks inside the skin but it is empty. "Where is my banana?" he asks Millie.

Millie opens her eyes wide with amazement and says: "Didn't you see? Well, I certainly did. The banana flew out of the skin when it fell out of the tree. Bananas can fly, didn't you know?"

Micky scratches behind his ear. It sounds funny to him. Flying bananas? Really? He picks up some leaves and begins to chew them. They're not half as nice as a banana.

Millie licks her lips contentedly as she thinks about the delicious banana. I hope Micky is just as silly next time, she thinks.

2 January

Monkey Jim

Can you see that monkey?
That is Monkey Jim.
He lives in very tall, high trees,
where friends can play with him.

He plays tag very often,
and swings from tree to tree.
He very nearly always wins,
"You never will catch me!"

By evening time he's tired,
snuggles up to mother's fur.
Our Monkey Jim is fast asleep,
all night he will not stir.

3 January

Pippy and Coco

Can you see that little monkey playing with the giraffe? That is Pippy. He is only a baby monkey, who mostly stays near his mother. But sometimes he's allowed to play with the other little monkeys. They play tag and hide and seek, and sometimes who can eat the most bananas. But Pippy really prefers playing with his friend. His friend is Coco the giraffe. Coco lets Pippy slide down his long neck. What fun!

4 January

A jacket for Jake

"Mother," says Alice, "Jake is cold. He shivers when I take him out to play
in the snow. I feel sorry for him."
Mother is worried. Jake mustn't catch a cold. "I've got a good idea," she says.
"There's still some material left from the jacket I made for you. Shall I make
a jacket for Jake, too?"
The next day, Jake's jacket is ready. Jake is lovely and warm, so Alice can
take him out to play in the snow.

5 January

Grandpa's glasses

Jake the toy monkey looks very silly. He is alone in the sitting room and is wearing glasses. Grandpa's glasses. Peter put them on him. Peter saw Grandpa's glasses just lying there on the table and decided to put them on Jake. So now Jake is looking through the glasses. Everything looks so funny! Everything that is close to him is enormous! The glasses are very good for Grandpa, because they help him to see the small letters in the newspaper. But they make Jake laugh. He'd like to keep the glasses. Then everything would always look funny. And he would like a beard and a pipe like Grandpa's, too.

6 January

Cato the monkey

Look, look inside the toy shop,
who's that sitting on the ground?
It's a little cuddly monkey,
Very pink, and soft, and round.

He needs someone to buy him,
and Cato is his name.
He'll give you great big cuddles,
if you will do the same.

7 January

Making a snow monkey

When the monkeys in the wood wake up in the morning, everything is white. The trees are white. The grass is white. It has been snowing. Timmy Monkey looks out of the window. "Oh, look!" he cries. "It's been snowing!" Timmy rushes outside. His monkey friends, Bob and Tom, are already there. "I've got a good idea," says Timmy. "Let's make a snow monkey." They make a snowball and roll it around in the snow. The snow sticks to the snowball and makes it bigger and bigger until it is big enough. "Right," says Bob, "this is his body." They make another ball of snow, but not quite so big. This is the head. They put the head onto the body. Tom fetches a broom and puts it under the snow monkey's arm. Then they look for small stones. These are going to be the eyes, nose, and buttons. The snow monkey is nearly finished. "It hasn't got any hair," says Timmy. So they all look for short twigs. There, finished! Golly, this does make you hungry, think the monkeys. They run home for something to eat. Goodbye, Mr Snow Monkey. See you tomorrow!

13

The monkey hairdresser

Jeremy Monkey thinks everything is fun.
Everything, that is, except going to the hairdresser's.
He hates it. "Jeremy!" calls his mother, "come on.
Time to have your hair cut."
"But I don't want my hair cut!" wails Jeremy.
"No buts," says Mother, "you've got to go. Your hair is
far too long. You won't be able to see anything soon."
At the hairdresser's, Jeremy has to sit on a chair.
The hairdresser puts a cape around him. "So, Jeremy,"
says the hairdresser, "shall I cut it nice and short all over?"
Jeremy begins to cry. "I don't want short hair.
I want long hair," he sniffs. The hairdresser feels a bit
sorry for Jeremy. But he says: "I see, but you won't be able
to see anything soon with all that long hair in front of
your eyes." Then he has an idea. From his pocket, he
takes a beautiful green ribbon. He ties up Jeremy's
long hair with the green ribbon. "There you are," he says,
"now you've got a lovely tail on your head. Your hair is still
long, but now you can see properly! And I don't need
to cut your hair, either."

9 January

Sledging

The wood is still covered by a thick layer of snow.
Eric and Ernie Monkey are going sledging. There is
a big hill in the wood. It is excellent to slide down on
a sledge. "I'm first!" shouts Ernie, and gets onto the
sledge. Whoosh! … Ernie slides all the way down
very quickly. Such fun.
"Now me!" cries Eric. He jumps on the sledge and,
whoosh, there he goes. But, oh dear, Eric is going very,
very fast, and there is a branch in his path. Eric can't
slow the sledge down. He keeps going faster and faster!
The branch gets closer and closer! Boom! The sledge
crashes into the branch. Eric flies through the air.
He lands on his head in a big snowdrift. All you can
see is the tip of his tail sticking out of the snow.
Luckily, Eric hasn't hurt himself. He scrabbles to get
out of the snow. "That was exciting," says Eric to
Ernie, "but I'd prefer not to crash next time!"

10 January

The monkey from Chad

There once was a monkey from Chad,
whose manner was awfully sad,
for his toes were too long,
yes, much, much too long,
so his walking was painful, quite bad.

But a doctor from far-off Korea,
said: "With long toes you've nothing to fear.
They'll be fixed in a jiffy,
with something quite niffy.
Those long toes will just disappear!"

So he made up a mixture, dark brown,
so smelly and niffy you'd frown.
But the terrible stink
made the too long toes shrink.
Now all's well for a walk about town.

15

11 January

Baking monkey cakes

Millie and Micky are at home on their own. They are a bit bored. "Let's make monkey cakes!" suggests Micky. "What a good idea," agrees Millie, "then we can surprise Mother." They go into the kitchen. Micky tries to get the flour out of the cupboard, but he can't quite reach. He jumps up onto the table, stretches up as high as he can, and just manages to get the flour. But oh dear! The table begins to wobble. Crash! Micky falls right on top of the eggs. He's got flour all over him, too. Micky is covered from head to tail in flour and eggs and looks a real mess. Millie got a fright, but begins to laugh. Micky looks so funny! Then their mother comes into the kitchen. "What has been going on here?" she asks. "We wanted to make monkey cakes to surprise you," says Micky. "I was trying to get the flour, but it was too high and then …" Micky doesn't know whether to laugh or cry. Luckily, Mother is not really cross. "I know," she says, "let's make monkey cakes together." So the three of them make a big pile of monkey cakes, and have no more surprises.

12 January

Skating on your hands

It is very cold outside. Everything is frozen. The pond in the wood is frozen over. "Are you coming skating, Ricky?" asks Joe Monkey. "You bet I am," says Ricky Monkey, "but I'm not very good at it yet."
"Doesn't matter, you'll learn," says Joe. So they go off to the pond together. There are lots of other monkeys on the ice already. Joe and Ricky put their skates on. Joe steps onto the ice. Whoosh! He's off and away. He is a good skater. But Ricky isn't. Every time he puts a foot on the ice he falls over. He just can't get going.
Then Ricky has an idea. "Joe!" he shouts, "lend me your skates for a minute."
Ricky fastens Joe's skates onto his monkey hands, and yes! He can do it! Ricky Monkey is skating on hands and feet. He doesn't fall over any more. What a clever monkey!

16

13 January

A riddle

Riddle me ree, riddle me ree,
a long tail and twinkly eyes you see.
Riddle me ree, riddle me ree,
bananas, bananas are best for me.

Riddle me ree, riddle me ree,
at jumping and climbing I'm good,
    you see.
Riddle me ree, riddle me ree,
can you guess who I'm talking about?
    (Tee hee!)

14 January

Grandpa's pipe

Grandpa Monkey is in the sitting room reading the newspaper.
Mischievous George Monkey is there, too. Grandpa lights his pipe.
"May I smoke a pipe, too, Grandpa?" asks George.
"Ahem," rumbles Grandpa, "pipe smoking is not for little
monkeys." And he goes back to his newspaper.
"Ring, ring," goes the doorbell. Grandpa gets up and goes to see
who is at the door. George looks mischievously at the pipe. I can
have a go now, he thinks. George picks up the pipe and sucks at it.
"Yeeuch," gasps George. It makes him cough. "That is disgusting!"
he says. Grandpa comes back into the room. He shakes his head
and says: "Silly George! Pipe smoking is not for little monkeys.
Pipe smoking is only for grandpa monkeys!"

15 January

Jacky is moving house

Jacky Monkey is moving house. Jacky doesn't like the idea one little bit. He has got lots of friends in the wood where he lives now. It's almost making Jacky cry. Here comes the removal van. Everything must be loaded into it. His bed, his toys, and lots of other things. When the van is full, they drive off. Jacky's mother has given him a banana. But he doesn't feel one bit like eating it. Then they arrive in the new wood. Jacky looks around. Oh, isn't it lovely here, he thinks. What a lot of bananas! And just look at the trees for climbing in! Look, there are some monkeys playing by that tree. Jacky goes over to them. He's not sad any more. He likes the new wood.

16 January

Monkey Fred

Have you heard the silly story
about funny Monkey Fred?
This silly little monkey
always stands upon his head.

Sometimes Father Monkey
starts to shout and wail:
"Why, you silly, silly monkey,
don't you sit upon your tail?"

Then silly Monkey Fred
sighs a very heavy sigh,
and says: "I like it better
with my legs so nice and high."

So, if you see a monkey
who is standing on his head,
there's no doubting whatsoever
that this is Monkey Fred.

17 January

The rain game

It is raining in the big wood. Big fat drops of water are falling from the sky. "I know a good game," says Micky Monkey to his sister Millie. "Let's catch raindrops!"

"How will you do that?" asks Millie.

"In my mouth!" says Micky. They run outside together. "You see those two trees over there, Millie?" says Micky. "We'll run from one tree to the other. When you're running, you must keep your mouth open and catch as many rain drops as you can."

Millie goes and stands under the tree. She opens her mouth. Then she runs to the other tree. One, two, three. She has caught three raindrops. "Now it's your turn, Micky," she says.

Micky opens his mouth, and begins to run. One, two, three, four, five … bang! Micky was running so fast he banged into the tree. Ow, that hurts! Micky rubs his chin. "But I did win," says Micky, "because I caught five raindrops and you only caught three."

"Yes," says Millie, "but I don't have a lump on my chin – you do!"

18 January

Monkey flu

Bob Monkey is in bed. He is ill. His throat hurts and he keeps coughing. The monkey doctor said that Bob must stay in bed, because he has got monkey flu. Bob doesn't like it at all. He would much prefer to be climbing a tree or playing outside with his friends. Worst of all, the doctor has given him some horrible medicine. Bob has to take two spoonfuls of this medicine each day. In the afternoon, his grandma comes to visit. She has brought Bob some bananas and coconuts. Bob is very pleased with his presents. When he has to take his medicine, he swallows it quickly, then eats a piece of banana straight away. It is much less horrid that way.

19 January

The monkey with the boat

A monkey made a boat one day,
out of a coconut shell.
It really was a lovely boat,
he'd built it rather well.

The mast was a stick in the middle,
the sail was an orange sock,
and when the wind began to blow,
the boat began to rock.

Along came Mr Elephant,
who said: "May I sail too?"
Oh no! He stepped into the boat
and broke it clean in two!

20 January

The monkey hut

Timmy and Tommy Monkey are standing under a large tree. "We could make a good monkey hut in this tree," says Timmy. "What a good idea," replies Tommy. They find some wood and branches and climb up into the tree. They use the wood and the branches to make the walls, then they get some leaves to make the roof. "Look," says Tommy to Timmy, "you can almost see the edge of the wood." Timmy stretches up onto his toes to get a better look. But, oh dear, he is standing too near the edge. Oops! Timmy falls out of the hut. He just manages to grab hold of a branch with his tail as he falls. That was close!

20

21 January

The strong fish

"Have you caught anything yet?" Millie asks her brother Micky.
"No, nothing," answers Micky. Millie and Micky are sitting on the
riverbank, fishing. They have each got a rod with a long line.
And on the line is a hook with a piece of banana on it. "Perhaps
fish don't like bananas!" says Micky. But then his rod begins to
move. "I've got a bite, I've got a bite!" he shouts. He tries to pull
the line with the fish out of the water. But the fish is much
stronger than Micky. Splosh! The fish has pulled Micky into the
water, fishing rod and all! Millie bursts out laughing. Micky looks
so funny, all wet and dripping. Micky doesn't think it's funny.
He puts a fresh piece of banana on his hook. "Just you wait, fish,"
he says, "I'll get you yet!"

22 January

The monkey in the west

There was a monkey in the West,
who was always being a pest.
If you shouted: "Give it a rest!"
he'd still continue being a pest.

Then along came an elephant,
who said: "Naughty thing!"
Use a bit of common sense,
and stop that pestering!

Or else I'm going to give you
a smack real good and hard.
I don't care if it hurts or not,
so you'd best be on your guard!"

23 January

Upside down world

Bob and Ernie Monkey are sitting in a tree together.
"Look what I can do!" says Ernie to Bob. "I'm very good at
hanging by my tail!" He curls his tail around a branch and
hangs upside down. "Golly," says Bob, "I'd like to have a
go at that, too." He curls his tail around the branch and …
it works! Bob is hanging upside down from the branch, too.
"Gosh," says Bob, "doesn't the wood look funny! It looks like
everything is the wrong way round. The trees, the bananas in
the trees, the grass, the sky … everything is standing on
its head. I like it! I think I'll hang here a bit longer."
Do you think Bob is still hanging on the branch?

24 January

An unhappy bird

Ellie and Nellie Monkey are out walking in the snow.
"Brr, it's cold!" says Nellie. Suddenly they hear a noise:
"Cheep, cheep." Ellie and Nellie look around. Where is
the noise coming from? "Cheep, cheep." There it is again.
Then they see who is making the noise. It is a little bird,
huddled up against a tree. The poor bird is terribly cold.
"What's the matter, little bird?" asks Ellie.
"Cheep, cheep," answers the bird, "I'm so cold and
I'm so hungry. Cheep, cheep."
"I know what we'll do," says Nellie, "we'll take you home
with us. You can warm yourself by the fire and have
something to eat." When they get home, Ellie and Nellie
give the little bird some bread and water while he sits in
front of the nice, warm fire.

25 January

Hello, I am Hunky

Hello, I am Hunky,
a nice little monkey,
I play and I laugh all day long.
I am William's toy
(he's a nice little boy),
And sometimes I sing him a song.
And, when it is time
(yes, you know what time),
when it's time to go upstairs to bed,
that nice little boy
says: "Favourite toy,
come and sleep with me here in my bed."

26 January

Writing a letter

Margaret Monkey is sitting at the table. She has a piece of paper and a pen. Do you know what she is doing? She is writing a letter. Margaret is writing a letter to Grandpa and Grandma Monkey. And do you know what she is writing? "Dear Grandpa and Grandma, how are you? I'm fine. May I come and stay with you one day? Lots of love, from Margaret." The letter is finished. Margaret puts the letter in an envelope and asks her mother for a stamp. Now she can send the letter. She puts the letter in the letter box. That's done then, she thinks. Margaret hopes that Grandma and Grandpa will answer her letter. And perhaps they will say that she may come to stay!

Playing mothers and fathers

Micky and Millie Monkey are in the sitting room.
"I know," says Millie, "let's play mothers and fathers."
"Fine," answers Micky, "I'll be the father and you can be the mother."
"Okay," says Millie, "but then we must look like Father and Mother."
Micky and Millie go to their mother and father's bedroom. The wardrobe
is full of real grown-up clothes. Millie puts on a very large dress. The dress is
really too big, but it doesn't matter. Then she puts on a pair of blue shoes
with high heels. Oops, it's a bit wobbly on high heels if you're not used to
them! Micky has got a pair of trousers and a jacket out of the wardrobe.
He puts them on. "You need a tie, too," says Millie, "then you will
look right." Micky finds a nice tie and knots it round his neck. Millie
and Micky go and look at themselves in the mirror. "Hee, hee, hee,"
laughs Millie, "you do look funny in those big clothes."
Micky is laughing, too. "You're so tall in those high heels!"
"Come on, Mother Monkey," says Micky to Millie, "let's go and
have a cup of coffee." "What an excellent idea, Father Monkey,"
she answers. And off they go.

28 January

The money-box

Timmy Monkey has been given a present. Guess what it is?
A great big money-box. And it's not just an ordinary money-box,
it's a very special one. It is a money-box shaped like an elephant.
An elephant with a trunk, a tail, four legs, and two big ears.
In between the ears, on top of his head, is a slot. That's where you
put the money in, so you can keep the money safe. That is called
saving. Each time Timmy is given a penny, he puts it in his money-
box. Timmy hopes to save a lot of money in his money-box.
Then he will be able to buy lots of nice things with the money.
How about a large banana ice-cream? Timmy dreams about
all the lovely things he can save up for.

29 January

Who do I see?

Who do I see?
No, that's not really me,
it can only be
smart Monkey Fred.
Brown jacket, pink tie,
white shirt and, oh my!
He's got a grand
hat on his head!
I'm off to see Grandma,
that's why I'm so smart,
I'm the smartest Fred
you'll ever see.
And if I can stay
clean and tidy all day,
I may be invited to tea.

30 January

Learning to ride a bicycle

Bobby Monkey has got a new bicycle. It is a beautiful red bicycle.
There is a bell on the handlebars. You can ring the bell to let
people know you are coming. But Bobby has never ridden a
bicycle. He still has to learn. And that's not easy. Bobby sits on
the saddle. He puts his monkey feet on the pedals but … oops,
he falls over! Here comes his father. He's come to help Bobby.
He holds the bicycle while Bobby gets on. Bobby pedals very
carefully. He doesn't fall any more, because Father is holding him.
And yes! The bicycle is moving forwards. Bobby goes faster
and faster. Then father lets go. And look! Bobby can do it all by
himself. Ring, ring. Bobby rings his bicycle bell. Look out,
here I come. And Bobby rides all around on his beautiful
new red bicycle.

31 January

A monkey sister

It is a very special day today. Do you know why? Because Nicky Monkey has got a new sister today. His mother had a very fat tummy. That was Nicky's little sister inside. She stayed there for a long, long time, because she had to grow big enough to be born. And today she is big enough, so she has come out of Mother's tummy. Nicky is very happy to have a baby sister. Father and Mother are very happy, too. The baby sister does look very tiny. She has tiny hands and feet, and a tiny little tail. She has got a lot of growing to do. She cries a bit, too. But that doesn't matter, because all babies cry. For the time being, Nicky will have to wait before he can teach her how to climb trees, because she is still far too small. Nicky and Father and Mother all thought up a name for the baby. Can you guess what they called her? Mary. Isn't that a pretty name?

1 February

Secret monkey language

Ellie and Nellie Monkey are sitting on the sofa in the sitting room.
"I've got an idea!" says Ellie. "Let's make up our own secret monkey
language!" "Secret monkey language?" asks Nellie. "What do you mean?"
"Well," says Ellie, "secret monkey language is a language that nobody else
can understand. Only us two. So we can talk to each other and no-one
will understand what we're saying."
"Is it very difficult?" asks Nellie.
"Not at all," replies Nellie. "It's really easy. We just decide that every word
we say has to begin with the letter B. So you could say: 'Good morning'
and it would sound like: 'Bood borning'. Do you understand what I
mean?" Nellie laughs. "It does sound funny, Ellie, but I understand.
So I should say: 'Bood borning bo bou, boo!' " Ellie and Nellie fall about
laughing. It really does sound funny, this secret monkey language.
Then their mother comes into the room. "Hello," she says.
"Bello," reply Ellie and Nellie together.
Mother looks surprised. What did they say? she thinks.
"Are you feeling all right?" she asks.
"Bes, bother," say Ellie and Nellie, laughing.
Mother doesn't understand a word.
But we do, don't we?

2 February

Mary Monkey

Now who was that
who just flew past?
I see her up that tree.
It must be Mary Monkey,
as quick as quick can be.

She's very good at climbing,
up, and down, and round.
Sometimes it really looks as if
her feet don't touch the ground.

But now she's getting tired,
she closes her eyes tight.
She snuggles down, she's fast asleep,
she'll sleep right through the night.

3 February

Picking coconuts

Timmy and his father are going coconut picking in the wood today.
They are walking along together. "Look," says Father, "there's a big palm tree."
Quick as a flash, they climb to the top. Father picks a coconut. But what's
he doing now? He's throwing it down to the ground.
"Boom!" goes the coconut as it crashes down. Hey, what a good game,
thinks Timmy. So he, too, picks a coconut and throws it down to the ground.
Then he throws two more. "Boom, boom!" But all this hard work makes
them very hungry. Father breaks open one of the coconuts and they eat it
up together. After all, they had earned it with all that hard work!

4 February

The drawing

It is raining. Large drops of rain are falling on the window. Annette is bored, because she can't play outside. Her toy monkey Abraham is sitting in front of her on the table. He looks a bit bored, too. "I know what you could do," says her mother, "you could do a drawing." "Yes," says Annette, "that is a good idea. I'm going to draw Abraham." Concentrating hard, Annette does the very best drawing she can of her toy monkey. Her drawing is so good that Mother pins it up on the wall. It is the best drawing Annette has ever done.

So you see, a rainy day once in a while is not such a bad thing after all!

5 February

The monkey from Guyana

Do you know the silly monkey,
who lives in the Guyanas?
Well, every single day he eats
one hundred ripe bananas!

Now, this has made him very fat,
or, if you wish, quite stout,
and with this big, fat tummy,
it's quite hard to get about.

So he just sits, and eats, and sits,
and eats lots more bananas.
I think that very soon he will
burst out of his pyjamas!

The kite

Henry Monkey is in a field. He is flying a kite. His grandpa gave him a splendid kite with a face on one side. The kite has a long tail with lots of red ribbons tied to it. And, so that Henry can hold onto it safely, the kite is attached to a long, long string. The wind keeps the kite in the air. Henry keeps tight hold of the string because the wind is strong. Suddenly, the wind blows the kite into a high tree. The string gets all tangled among the leaves and branches. Henry climbs into the tree to get the kite. He is very lucky that it isn't broken. Henry takes the kite off to a different part of the field where there are no trees. Getting his kite caught in a tree once is quite enough for Henry.

7 February

Hide and seek

Micky and Millie Monkey are playing hide and seek. Millie puts her hands in front of her eyes and begins to count. "One, two …" Micky hides quickly. He knows an excellent hiding place. "… three, four, five!" counts Millie. "I'm coming!" Where could Micky be? Millie looks under the sofa, under the chair, and under the table. She looks in the kitchen and in the bedroom. Then she goes to the hall. She doesn't see anything, but she does hear a noise. "Peekaboo!" Millie turns round. Where did that noise come from? She can't see anything. "Peekaboo!" Millie looks at the coat stand where all the coats are hanging. Coats can't talk, can they? she thinks. But then one of the coats moves slightly. So that's where Micky is! "Golly, you'd found a good hiding place," says Millie, "but I found you after all!"

8 February

The big balloon

Eric and Ernie Monkey are out for a walk in the
wood. "Oh look, look up there!" says Ernie.
He's pointing up into the sky. Eric looks
upwards. "What do you think it is?"
he asks Ernie. "It looks like a balloon."
"It is a balloon," replies Ernie, "a very big
balloon. Can you see the basket hanging
underneath it? You can get in it and fly
over the wood. Look, there's someone
in it now!" They look at the basket
and see somebody waving at them.
Hello! Eric and Ernie wave back.
"I'd like to do that, too,"
says Ernie. "Perhaps when
I'm grown up."

9 February

Fire in the wood

When Millie and Micky Monkey are walking through the wood, they smell a strange
smell. "Can you smell it, too?" Micky asks Millie. "Yes, I can," she answers. "It smells
like fire." "Look, over there!" shouts Micky. "That tree's on fire!" "Oh no!" says Millie,
frightened. "Whatever shall we do, Micky?" "We must fetch water," replies Micky,
"lots of water. Then we might be able to put out the fire." Millie and Micky quickly
get some buckets and run to the lake to fill them with water. They rush back to the
burning tree and throw the buckets of water over it. Sssss, goes the fire and goes out.
"We were only just in time," says Micky. "The tree isn't badly burned."

10 February

The monkey from Runnymede

Now, once there was a monkey,
who lived in Runnymede.
At singing he was very good,
extremely good indeed.

But just before his song he sang,
that monkey, with a grin,
would place his hat upon the ground,
for throwing money in.

11 February

The playground

Jessica Monkey is going to the playground with her grandpa today. Jessica makes
straight for the see-saw. She sits on one end and Grandpa sits on the other.
See-saw, see-saw. But, oh no! Jessica is wobbling and … falls off onto the ground!
Ow, ow, that hurts! Jessica starts to cry. She's got a bump on her head.
"I know," says Grandpa, "let's go and get an ice-cream. Then you'll feel much better."
Jessica is allowed to choose a great big ice-cream. Mmm, delicious. She forgets
all about the bump on her head.

12 February

The monkey dentist

Ricky Monkey is a bit nervous. He's got to go to the monkey dentist. His mother goes with him. "Hello, Ricky," says the dentist. "How are you? Have you been brushing your teeth?" Ricky nods his head. "And I hope you haven't been eating too many sweets." Ricky shakes his head.

"Good," says the dentist, "you can sit in the chair now." Ricky climbs into the big dentist's chair. "Right," says the dentist, "open your mouth, Ricky." The dentist looks inside Ricky's mouth with a small mirror. That way he can get a good look at all Ricky's teeth. "That looks fine to me," says the dentist, "not even one hole. Well done!" Thank goodness, thinks Ricky with relief. "You can close your mouth now, Ricky," says the dentist, "I've finished. See you next time!" Ricky isn't frightened any more. "Goodbye, Mr Dentist," he says, "see you next time, too!"

13 February

Tom Monkey can't sleep

Tom Monkey is in bed. He can't sleep. It is his birthday tomorrow, and he is so excited thinking about the presents he is going to get that he lies there wide awake. What will he get? Perhaps a ball, or a car. Or maybe a toy train, or it might be a new bicycle. Tom just doesn't know. And he's having a party in the afternoon. All his friends are invited. But what will they bring him? An exciting book or a game or … or … or …
Tom falls asleep. All that thinking about presents has made him tired. Now Tom is dreaming about his birthday and all the presents. Night, night, Tom! See you in the morning!

14 February

The monkey from London Town

Now, once there was a monkey,
who came from London Town.
And what do you think? That monkey
wished he were a clown!

He found a pair of giant shoes,
(the kind with flappy toes),
a baggy suit of yellow and green,
a tomato on his nose.

He'd pull such funny faces
as he fell about the place.
The people really loved to see
his funny, monkey face.

15 February

A snowball down your neck

It is winter in the wood. Snow and ice are everywhere. Millie Monkey is looking for her brother Micky. "Micky, Micky," she shouts, "where are you?" All of a sudden, she hears a swishing noise coming towards her. It's a snowball. The snowball lands right on her neck. Brrr, that's cold! Then Millie hears someone laughing. Micky.
"Ha, ha," laughs Micky, "I got you there!"
But Millie isn't laughing. A snowball down your neck is cold and horrible.
Very carefully, Millie picks up a handful of snow and makes it into a ball. Micky doesn't notice. Millie goes up to Micky. "Very funny, I don't think," says Millie.
"Oh yes, it was!" says Micky with a grin. "The best bit was, that you didn't see it coming!" Just as Micky begins to laugh again, Millie stuffs her snowball down his neck. Micky jumps with fright. Brrr, whatever is that? It's very cold.
Now it's Millie's turn to laugh. "That was good, wasn't it? A snowball down your neck," says Millie. "And the best bit was, you didn't see it coming!"

16 February

Annoying Aunt Monkey

Robbie Monkey looks a bit glum. His aunt is coming to visit and Robbie doesn't like it one little bit. He has to get dressed up in smart clothes and shoes. And she always gives him a kiss on his cheek. A kiss isn't so bad, but she wears funny lipstick that rubs off on your cheek. Yuck!

"Ring, ring!" Is that the doorbell? No, it's the telephone. Robbie picks up the receiver.

"Hello, this is Robbie speaking," he says.

"Hello, Robbie, this is Aunt Monkey. Would you please tell your mother that I won't be able to come today?" she says.

"Oh yes," answers Robbie, "I'll tell her." Robbie puts the telephone down.

"Mother," he says, "Aunt Monkey can't come today."

"Oh, what a shame," says Mother.

"Yes, a real shame," says Robbie. But he doesn't really think it's a shame at all. Now he can go and play outside.

17 February

Wibble wobble tooth

Once there was a monkey,
who lived on chocolate mousse,
and one fine day, to his great delight,
he found that a tooth was loose.

That tooth he could wobble
(great wobbles, or small).
It was funny to watch him.
Did it hurt? Not at all!

18 February

Away visiting

Frederick Monkey is going on a visit to his grandma and grandpa. He will stay there
for two nights and then go home. His father takes him in the car. When they get to
Grandma and Grandpa's house, Father toots the horn. "Toot, toot!" Frederick gets out
of the car with his suitcase. Grandma is there, waiting for him. "Hello, Frederick,"
she says. "Nice to see you!" Father turns the car round and goes back home.
"Bye, Father!" shouts Frederick. "See you in two days!"
"Bye, Frederick," shouts Father, "have a nice time, and be good!"
"But you're always good," says Grandma with a laugh.
"Yes," says Frederick, "I am!" Grandma and Frederick have a good laugh together.

19 February

Knocking down tin cans

The fair has come to the wood. There are bumper-cars, a roundabout, and lots of different games to play. One of the games is knocking down tin cans. Tim and Tom Monkey are having a competition: whoever knocks down the most tin cans gets a prize. There is a pile of five tin cans and the idea is to knock them down with a ball. Tom goes first. He throws the ball very hard. He knocks down two tin cans. He has another go. "Boom!" and knocks down one more tin can. Tom has knocked down three tin cans. Now it is Tim's turn. He aims at a new pile of tin cans. "Boom, boom, boom!" Tim throws the ball so hard that three tin cans fall to the ground. Tim still has another go. And, yes! He knocks down the other two tin cans. Tim has knocked them all down. So he has won. He may choose his prize. He takes a large banana and breaks it in two. One piece for himself and the other for Tom. So they both have something. Mmm, what a delicious prize.

20 February

Playing nurse

Millie and Micky Monkey are playing in the sitting room. Millie is the nurse and Micky is the patient. "Hello, nurse," Micky says to Millie, "my arm hurts."
"Yes, I see," says nurse Millie, "you've got a broken arm."
"What are you going to do, nurse?" asks Micky.
"Well," says Millie, "I'll have to bandage it." Nurse Millie gets the first aid box and takes out a large bandage. She wraps the bandage around Micky's arm, but she doesn't stop there! She goes on to bandage his other arm, head, and legs, too! Micky is bandaged from head to toe. He does look funny. "Thank you very much, nurse," says Micky, "until the next time!" Millie and Micky think it's all very funny, and fall about laughing.

21 February

The painted monkey

Somewhere far off in monkeyland,
a long, long way from here,
there lives a little monkey,
who does a thing that's queer.

He paints himself all over,
in red, green, blue, and yellow.
Some purple spots are added,
he's such a funny fellow.

Now, this funny, painted monkey
will make you laugh, not frown.
He says: "This is much better
than boring, boring brown!"

22 February

The noises game

"I know a good game," says Ellie to Sally. "I'll make an animal noise and you have to guess which animal it is." "Fine," replies Sally, "but don't make it too difficult, will you?" "No," says Ellie, "I'll begin with an easy one. Miaow, miaow." "I know!" shouts Sally, "that's a cat!" "Correct," says Ellie. "Now this one: squeak, squeak." "That's a mouse," says Sally. Now it's her turn. "Moo," she says. Ellie knows this one. It is a cow. "I know another one," says Sally. "Glug, glug, glug." Ellie has to think about this one. "It's a fish!" she shouts. "Now it's my turn again," says Ellie. But she doesn't say anything. Sally thinks hard. What could it be? Which animal makes no noise at all? Ellie laughs. "It was Jock, my toy monkey!" That's not fair, thinks Sally, Jock isn't a real animal.

42

23 February

Wet feet

Bobby Monkey takes a run up and jumps right in the middle of a puddle. It isn't a very deep puddle, but the water splashes everywhere. Bobby does another big jump. The water splashes all over the place again. This really is fun, thinks Bobby, as I have got my boots on. He carries on jumping in all the puddles he can find. But then what happens? Oh dear, Bobby jumps in the next puddle. It is a very deep one. Splosh! Bobby is up to his knees in water and his feet are soaking wet. Bobby squelches his way out of the puddle. He takes off his boots and turns them upside down. Lots of water comes out of them and makes another puddle at his feet!

24 February

Too much banana cake

Frank Monkey is sitting on the sofa. He has got a tummy ache and it is his own fault. Do you know why? Because he ate a whole banana cake! The banana cake was on the kitchen table. At first, Frank thought: I'll just try a small piece, to see if I like it. Then he took another piece, and then another, and then another … until the whole cake was gone! The tummy ache will go away. But I don't think Frank will ever eat a whole banana

Amy's game

Have you ever heard
of a little girl called Amy?
This little girl
knows a nice little game.

Each evening as she goes to bed,
she says goodnight to all:
her toys, the window, and the door,
and even, "Goodnight, wall!"

"I'm going to go to sleep now,
and hold my monkey tight.
so Goodnight everybody,
and everything, Goodnight!"

26 February

A house on your back?

"Look at that funny thing," says Hunky Monkey to his friend Tom. "It is brown and grey. It looks like a small animal. And it moves very, very slowly."

"That's a snail," says Tom. "Snails go very slowly. That's because they carry their house on their backs. They take it everywhere with them. And then, if the snail wants to go to sleep, or if it starts to rain, it can just creep into its house."

"That's odd," says Hunky. "When I want to go to bed, I have to go home first."

"Yes, me too," says Tom, "but not this snail. He's always got his house with him wherever he goes. It's quite convenient, really. He can sleep wherever he wants to."

"I still think it's a bit strange," says Hunky.

"Well, yes, I suppose so," replies Tom, "strange but handy!"

27 February

Blowing bubbles

Edward and John are playing in the garden. They are blowing bubbles. "I've got a good one," calls out Edward. The soap bubble floats in the air, higher and higher. Then it bursts. John tries, too. But guess what happens? The soap bubble lands on the head of Pino, the toy monkey. It does look funny. Edward starts to laugh. "Ha, ha, look at you, Pino. You've got a bubble on your head! You'd better be careful, or you'll take off and float up into the sky!" Plop! The bubble bursts. "Oh, what a shame!" says Edward. "Let's try again." Both of them try to land another soap bubble on Pino's head.

28 February

A special sticking plaster

Jimmy Monkey is up at the top of a tree. Suddenly he hears his mother calling him. "Jimmy, Jimmy, supper's ready!" He climbs down a bit too quickly and scrapes his knee on the way. Ow, that hurts! It's bleeding a bit, too. It makes Jimmy cry. He walks home very carefully. Mother fetches a sticking plaster, a very special one with a coloured picture on it. Jimmy is very happy with the special sticking plaster on his knee. The knee doesn't hurt so much any more.
"Come on then," says Mother, "let's eat!" And Jimmy forgets all about his hurt knee.

A lost eye

Alice is sad. Jake, her toy monkey, is broken.
The horrible boy from next door did it. Alice was
playing outside with Jake yesterday when the boy
from next door grabbed him. He kicked him high
into the air. Poor Jake landed right in the middle of
a puddle. Alice took him home and put him on a
radiator to dry. But then she noticed that he had
lost an eye. So now poor Jake looks at her very
mournfully with his one eye.
"Alice, come downstairs, I've got something for you!"
calls her mother. Alice picks up Jake, gives him a
kiss, and goes downstairs. "Look," says Mother,
"I've bought Jake a new eye. I'll sew it on after
you've gone to bed."
Alice gives Mother a great big hug.
Tomorrow Jake will be able to face the
world with two eyes again!

1 March

Isobel writes her own name

Isobel is sitting at the table. She has got a piece of paper and a pen.
Isobel is writing. She is writing her own name. Isn't Isobel clever?
She already goes to school. Isobel has learnt how to write her name
at school. It's not easy, learning how to write. But it's not too
difficult either. You have to practise a lot. First you learn one letter.
When you know that one, you learn another. And another. And
another, until you know them all. Isobel could already write a bit
before she went to school. Mother had taught her. First her name,
then the name Curly. Curly is Isobel's cuddly monkey.
Curly is sitting next to Isobel. He's watching Isobel write her name.
When she has finished, she says: "Look, Curly, that is your name.
I've written it down." It really looks as if Curly is smiling. I bet he
likes having his name written down on a piece of paper.

2 March

Theo and Leo make music

"Boom, boom, boomperdeboom. Boom, boom, boomperdeboom!" What on earth is that noise? Oh look, it's Theo Monkey. He's playing a drum. It is a lovely blue drum, which is hanging round his neck. Theo has two drumsticks in his hands. One in each hand. "Boom, boom, boomperdeboom." Theo is enjoying the music he is making. "Toot, toot, tootadetoot!" What is this other noise now? It's Leo Monkey. He's playing a flute. Theo and Leo are making music together. What fun! Can you hear them? "Boom, boom, boomperdeboom, toot, toot, tootadetoot!"

3 March

A kiss for the moon

What does Ricky Monkey do,
    before he goes to sleep?
He opens wide the curtains,
    and at the moon does peep.

"I would so really love to give
    the moon and stars a kiss.
But they're so very far away,
I'll blow them one, like this!"

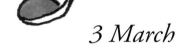

4 March

Together in the bath

"Hey you, stop splashing me!" says Millie Monkey to her brother Micky. "I've got soap in my eyes because of you." Millie and Micky are in the bath. The bath water is lovely and warm with lots of bubbles.

"Look at me," says Micky. He puts a dollop of bubbles on his head. It looks just like a hat. A bubble hat.

"That's fun," says Millie, "I'm going to do it, too!" Millie puts some bubbles on her head, just like Micky. "Shall we make some more bubbles?" asks Millie.

"Yes, good idea," replies Micky. He gets the bottle of bubble bath. Oh no! The bottle is very slippery with soap. It falls in the water with a great splash! Micky tries to get hold of the bottle, but he can't. More and more bubbles keep appearing in the bath – so many bubbles, in fact, that you can't see Micky and Millie any more. Just the tips of their tails stick out above the bubbles. Then Mother Monkey comes into the bathroom. "What is going on here?" she asks. "All I can see is bubbles." Mother gets rid of the bubbles. And laughs. She isn't cross. "Come on now, you two, out of the bath," says Mother. "I should think you're clean by now!"

51

5 March

Reading is fun

Tim is reading a book with a lot of pictures in it. Tim can't really read yet, but he can look at pictures. There is a monkey in one of the pictures in the book. The monkey is having an adventure. He goes on a journey and meets lots of different animals. A hippopotamus and a crocodile, a giraffe, and a rhinoceros. The pictures show that the monkey's adventure is very exciting. What fun! Tim would like to have an adventure himself.

6 March

Simon does a painting

Simon is doing a painting with lots of paint. All different colours of paint. Red, yellow, blue, green, and purple. He is painting with a brush. But what shall he paint? A house, or a tree? Or a child with a scooter? No, Simon is going to paint monkeys, a whole picture full of monkeys. When the picture is finished, he's going to hang it on the wall in his room. Then he can look at it as often as he likes.

7 March

Two big ears

Do you know, there is a monkey
with ears that stick right out?
So big that every smallest sound
he hears, without a doubt.

He can hear when ants are dancing,
he can hear a purring cat,
he can even hear grass growing.
Now what do you think of that?

He can hear when flowers open,
he can hear whatever's said.
He can hear what Mother says,
except for: "Time for bed!"

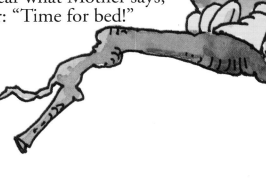

8 March

Bulbs in the garden

When Janey Monkey wakes up in the morning, it is beautiful weather. The sun is shining. Winter is nearly over. Janey gets dressed quickly and runs outside. She's going to see if there are any flowers in the garden yet. Before winter began, Janey planted some flower bulbs in the garden. Now spring is here, everything starts to grow, even the bulbs under the ground. Janey can see some green shoots poking out of the ground. These will grow into beautiful flowers in all different colours.

9 March

Margaret gets a letter

Margaret goes to the letter box by the garden gate. She hopes there will be a letter in it. A letter from Grandma and Grandpa. Yes, there is a letter! She runs inside quickly and reads it. It is from Grandma and Grandpa. Do you know what they wrote? "Dear Margaret, would you like to come and stay with us soon? Then we could all go to the zoo to see the monkeys. Lots of love, from Grandma and Grandpa." Margaret sits down straight away. She writes back to Grandma and Grandpa that she would love to come and stay.

10 March

A big fish?

Ricky and Jacob Monkey are sitting by the stream. They are both holding fishing-rods. They are fishing. "Have you caught anything, yet?" Ricky asks Jacob.
"No," says Jacob, "absolutely nothing."
"Wait a minute," says Ricky, "I think I feel something. Look, the float is going down. I've got a bite! Golly, it's really heavy. Help me, Jacob, I can't hold it on my own." They both pull hard on the fishing-rod … and fall over backwards in the grass. But it isn't a fish they've caught. No, Ricky and Jacob have caught an old boot!

11 March

The clothes monkey

There once was a monkey,
who had a silver dollar.
This monkey wore a coat,
with a very high collar.

He wore three pairs of trousers,
and five jumpers, so I'm told,
and seven pairs of woolly socks,
some thick, some thin, all old.

But if you asked that monkey:
"Why all these clothes?" he'd say:
"Why! To keep me nice and warm,
I'm warmer than you all day!"

12 March

Rhyming

Jeremy and Danny Monkey are in the sitting room. "I know a game," says Jeremy,
"it's called rhyming." "Rhyming?" asks Danny. "What does that mean?"
"Well," says Jeremy, "I say a word and you have to say a word that sounds like it. If I
say sheep, then you say sleep. Sleep rhymes with sheep. If I say house, you say mouse.
I'll begin," he says. "Grass." "Erm … glass," says Danny. "On my leg," says Jeremy.
"Is a peg!" says Danny. "Now it's my turn. I'm going to scream." "Peaches and cream,"
says Jeremy. Danny and Jeremy fall about laughing. They carry on with their game
and think up lots more rhyming words. Can you think of any good rhymes?

13 March

Cuddlemonkey is lost

Jenny has got a cuddly toy. It is a monkey, her cuddly monkey. Jenny takes the cuddly monkey everywhere with her. When Jenny goes to bed, Cuddlemonkey goes to bed, too. And when Jenny goes outside to play, Cuddlemonkey goes outside with her. But now something dreadful has happened. Cuddlemonkey has disappeared. Jenny can't find him anywhere. She has looked everywhere. She's so upset she's nearly crying. "What's the matter, Jenny?" asks Mother. "Why are you so upset?"
"I can't find Cuddlemonkey!" she wails. "Come on now," says Mother, "I'll help you look for him. Have you looked everywhere?" "Yes," answers Jenny, "everywhere." "In your bedroom?" asks Mother. "And under your bed?" Jenny stops and thinks. "I don't think so," she says. "Right," says Mother, "let's go and look together." Jenny looks under the bed. And who's that lying there? Cuddlemonkey! Do you think he was hiding?

14 March

Digger the mole

Frank Monkey is sitting on the grass.
He's looking at the ground. Suddenly,
the ground begins to move. What could
that be? A pile of soil appears on the
grass, and out of the pile of soil appears
a head. Frank doesn't understand.
Whatever could it be? "Hello," says the
head from the pile of soil, "who are you?
I'm Digger. Digger the mole."
"Digger the mole?" says Frank.
"Where have you come from?"
"I live under the ground," says the mole.
"That's where my house is. I dig long
tunnels under the ground, too. And
every now and again, I come up to the
surface for a look around. But I must
get on, I've a lot to do. Goodbye,
Frank. Until the next time."

15 March

The tiny monkey

Once there was a monkey,
no bigger than my thumb.
No monkey clothes would fit him,
which made him rather glum.

His mother bought a ball of wool,
and knitted him a coat,
a sweater, trousers, and some gloves,
a scarf for round his throat.

57

16 March

The geese return

"Look up at the sky," says Tim to his toy monkey. "Those are geese up there, flying in the sky. They have been to a warm country, because the winter here is too cold for them. They can't stand the cold as we can. We can put on warm clothes when it's cold, and you've got a lovely warm coat of fur. Now they're returning, because the weather is getting warmer. Isn't that nice?" The toy monkey nods his head. He thinks it's nice, too, that the geese are coming back.

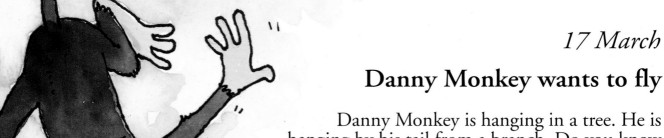

17 March

Danny Monkey wants to fly

Danny Monkey is hanging in a tree. He is hanging by his tail from a branch. Do you know what he is doing? He is trying to fly. Danny flaps his arms. Slowly at first, then faster and faster. But he doesn't seem to be having much success. Then along comes Jeremy Monkey. "What are you doing?" he asks. "I'm trying to fly," answers Danny. "Fly?" says Jeremy, "but you're not a bird, and you haven't got wings!"
"So that means I won't be able to fly?" asks Danny.
"No, of course you won't be able to fly, you silly monkey!" says Jeremy.

18 March

Minnie Monkey and the bee

"Bzzzz!" Whatever is that noise, thinks Minnie Monkey, and looks around her. What did she hear? There it is again. "Bzzzz!" Oh look! It's a bee. Minnie Monkey looks at the bee. It is a very large bee. It has yellow and black stripes on its body.

The bee flies to a flower and lands on it. The bee collects the nectar from the flower so it can turn this into honey. Minnie looks at the bee on the flower. She thinks it looks nice. Look, now the bee is flying away. It's going to another flower. Then to another, and then another. It carries on until it has found enough food. When it has enough, it flies back home to the beehive. At home in the beehive, the bees make honey from all the nectar they have found. And we can eat this honey. It is nice and sweet. Minnie loves honey. And what about you? Do you like honey?

19 March

The monkey from Leeds

There is a clever monkey,
who lives in Leeds.
A very clever monkey,
who reads and reads.

He can count up to a hundred,
and knows all his letters, too.
He's learnt them all so very well,
if he can, so can you!

So, look, and learn, and listen,
and one day you will know,
more than that smart monkey.
You will! (He told me so.)

20 March

When I'm grown up

Sam and Simon are lying on their backs on the grass. "When I'm grown up, I'm going to be a pilot," says Sam. "And when I'm grown up," says Simon, "I'm going to join the circus and be a monkey-tamer. I'll teach them lots of difficult tricks. And then everybody will clap." Sam thinks about this for a while. "That sounds like fun to me, too," he says, "everybody clapping. Perhaps I'll be an animal-tamer, too."

60

21 March

Spring

Jenny is out for a walk with her doll's pram. It is beautiful weather, because today is the first day of spring. The sun is shining and the birds are singing merrily. All that walking in the sunshine makes Jenny a bit hot. Should she take her coat off? Yes, why not? She takes off her coat and puts it down on the doll's pram. "I bet you're warm, too," she says to her doll Lucy and to Cuddlemonkey. "You've got a blanket over you, too. You must be far too hot. I know. You can both sit on my coat, then you'll be able to see better, too." Jenny walks on a bit further. She sings a little song. A little while later, she feels hot again. She wonders if she should take her jumper off, too. Why not, she thinks, the sun is shining so brightly. She takes Lucy's and Cuddlemonkey's jumpers off, too. When Jenny gets home, Mother says: "Jenny, what were you thinking of? It's not that warm yet! Put that jumper back on right now, and I think Lucy and Cuddlemonkey are a bit cold, too." Cuddlemonkey winks secretly at Jenny. He was quite happy without his jumper.

22 March

New clothes

If there's one thing that Gerry Monkey really hates, it's shopping for clothes. You have to try them on in a changing room. This is a small room with a curtain instead of a door. When you're in the changing room, you try on a pair of trousers to see if they fit. Gerry absolutely detests trying clothes on in a changing room. But you do need to try clothes on before you buy them. If something is too small, it's no good at all. Gerry is always pleased when they've finished and bought the clothes. Then it's time to go and have a drink somewhere with his mother. She usually lets him choose a cake, too. And then they go home.

23 March

Maria's monkey

Maria has a monkey, a very sweet, cuddly, soft monkey. Maria gives her monkey a bath every day. Then they have a cup of tea together. Delicious banana tea out of real cups. Then they have a cake as well. Maria's monkey isn't just sweet, he's very special. Can you guess why? Because he can talk. When you move him, he says: "My name is Jacko." At the end of the day, Maria takes Jacko to bed. "Night, night," says Maria, "see you in the morning." Night, night, Maria. See you in the morning!

24 March

The monkey from France

There once was a monkey
from France,
A quite foolish fellow,
it's said.

He wears his trousers
back to front.
Do you think he has gone
off his head?

25 March

Our own names

"Grandpa," asks Tim Monkey, "has everybody got a name?" "I think so," says Grandpa. "What's your name then?" asks Tim. "My real name is William," answers Grandpa, "but you call me Grandpa." "Why does everybody have a name?" Tim wants to know. "Well," says Grandpa, "if we didn't all have our own names, we'd all just be called Monkey. And then how would you know who is who? If I want to call you and shout 'Monkey, come here,' not just you would come, but so would twenty others. It would be rather awkward." Tim laughs. "It would be very funny," he says, "but not very handy. So it is a good idea after all that we all have our own names."

You pair of naughty monkeys!

Millie and Micky Monkey are in the sitting room. "Shall we play hairdressers?" says Millie. "Yes, that would be fun," says Micky. "I'm the hairdresser," says Millie, "and you are the customer." They find some clothes to dress up in.

Micky sits on a chair. Millie gets the scissors. "Not too short, please, hairdresser!" says Micky. "No, sir," says Millie. Very carefully, Millie cuts off a piece of Micky's hair. Then she cuts another, and then another.

"Does it look nice, hairdresser?" asks Micky. "Oh yes, sir," says Millie, "it looks very nice indeed." Micky isn't quite sure. "May I have a look in the mirror?" he asks. "Certainly, sir," says Millie, "here is the mirror." Micky looks at himself in the mirror. "What have you done?" he asks. "It's all crooked. And there are bits missing." Millie laughs. "You do look funny. I think it's gone a bit wrong."

Then Mother comes into the room. "What are you two up to now?" she asks crossly. "You pair of naughty monkeys," she says, "give me those scissors." She trims Micky's hair to make it straight again. Millie and Micky have to promise that they will never play hairdressers again. Ever.

27 March

Kittens

Something very special has happened today. Ricky Monkey's cat has had kittens. Three baby kittens. Two of them are black and white, and one is ginger. They are still very small. They have tiny ears and tiny tails. Ricky is very pleased with the kittens. They are so sweet. The best part is that Ricky is allowed to keep one of the kittens. The other two will be given to someone else. Ricky thinks he will probably keep the ginger kitten. He thinks it is the nicest.

28 March

The sandcastle

There once was a monkey
from far Swaziland,
and that little monkey
liked playing with sand.

He made a sandcastle,
and this castle it gives
him a place of his own,
and in it he lives.

He's vowed he will never
move house any more.
So this little monkey
is king of the shore!

29 March

The clay monkey

Sarah is sitting at the table. She is playing with clay. She was given the clay for her birthday. Now she's making something nice with it. She's making a monkey. It's quite difficult to make a monkey from clay, but Sarah is very good at it. The monkey is nearly finished. The clay is still soft. When the clay hardens, the monkey will be finished properly. Sarah is going to give the monkey to Mother. Mother will put it on a shelf. Then Sarah and Mother can look at it together.

30 March

Spot on your nose

When cheeky Chimpy Monkey
got out of bed one day,
he found a spot upon his nose,
grown there since yesterday.

"Wherever had it come from?
It isn't very nice,
I really feel an awful fool,
I think I'll close my eyes.

"For when I cannot see it,
it might just disappear."
He might be right, he might be wrong
(the latter's true, I fear).

31 March

Yuck, sprouts

Joshua is sitting at the table with his mother and father. They are eating.
They are eating something Joshua doesn't like: sprouts.
"Come on now, Joshua, eat up," says Father.
"But I don't like sprouts," says Joshua. "You must eat something, Joshua," says Mother.
"I have eaten something," he answers. "I've eaten all my potatoes and my meat.
I'm not hungry any more." "You have to eat some sprouts, Joshua," says Father.
"Yuck, sprouts," says Joshua, pulling a face. "I hate sprouts."
"You'll sit at this table until you've finished every single sprout," says Father.
Mother feels a bit sorry for Joshua. "Oh, how silly of me. What a mistake to make,"
says Mother suddenly. "These aren't sprouts at all. They're monkey kale and they taste
quite different from sprouts. Haven't you tried them yet, Joshua?"
Joshua takes a mouthful. Yes, Mother is right, he thinks. This tastes nice,
it's monkey kale, after all, not yucky sprouts. "Please may I have some more?"
says Joshua. "I like them!"

1 April

A joke

"Oh look!" says Micky Monkey to Millie Monkey. "You've got a frog in your hair!" "Eek!" squeals Millie. She puts her hand up to her hair and feels around for the frog. All she can feel is her hair and her ribbon. "Where, where's the frog?" she asks Micky. "April fool!" says Micky. "How silly," says Millie. She had completely forgotten that today was 1 April. On 1 April, or April Fool's Day, as it is called, the idea is to make jokes or trick people. Micky is good at that. Millie really thought that there was a frog in her hair.
"Well, Micky," says Millie, "I think I prefer the frog to the great big rip in your trousers. Mother will not be very pleased with you."
"Where? Have I really got a rip in my trousers?" says Micky.
"Where is it?" He looks at his trousers.
"Ha, ha, got you!" says Millie,
"April fool!"

2 April

I spy with my little eye

Josie and Peter are in the garden. "I know a good game," says Josie. "I spy with my little eye, something beginning with T. You have to guess what I mean." Peter looks around. What begins with T in the garden? "Tulip?" he suggests, but that's not right. Then Peter sees what it is: "Trousers," he says, "toy monkey's trousers!" Yes, he's right. Now it's Josie's turn to guess. What a good game!

3 April

The spider's web

"Look," says Hunky Monkey to his friend Tom, "can you see that spider's web? I wonder how a spider makes a web." "I know," says Tom. "The spider spins a sticky thread. He keeps on spinning this thread until he's spun lots and lots that meet in the middle. Then he makes a circle in the middle and keeps on going round and round and the circle gets bigger and bigger. Then the spider waits for a fly to fly into his web. When the web vibrates even a little, the spider knows that he has caught a fly."
"Golly," says Hunky, "what a clever spider!"

4 April

Alone no more

Once there was a monkey,
all by himself alone.
The others all had lots of friends,
but he'd not even one!

"I'll have to look around," he said,
"and see who I can find.
I don't mind fat, or tall, or thin,
as long as they are kind."

And then, at last, he found one.
His head was in a whirl.
So now he's got the bestest friend,
the best in all the world.

5 April

Peacock, peacock, I'm more beautiful than you

"Peacock, peacock, I'm more beautiful than you!"
"What are you doing?" Kathy Monkey asks
Davey Monkey. "I'm talking to the peacock,"
says Davey. "Can you see that big bird over there?
That is a peacock. It has a lovely tail with lots of
beautiful feathers in it. Its tail is down now, so
you can't really see how beautiful it is. I'm telling
the peacock that I'm more beautiful than it is in
the hope that it will lift up his tail to show who
is really the more beautiful. Kathy joins in and,
yes, the peacock lifts up its tail. Davey and
Kathy get a very good look at the beautiful tail.
Can you see it, too?

71

6 April

Sandwiches

Peter and Ellie are sitting at the table. They both have a peanut-butter sandwich in front of them. Maria's monkey, Jacko, is sitting next to them, just looking. He is hungry, too. Ellie says: "Would you like a bite, Jacko? Or would you like a whole sandwich?" Jacko just sits there and looks. He doesn't say anything. Ellie very carefully puts a crumb of bread and peanut-butter in Jacko's mouth. "Thank you very much," says Jacko, "I enjoyed that!"

7 April

Painting eggs

Peter and Ellie are allowed to paint eggs. It's fun to do, but you have to be very careful. The eggs break very easily. Ellie is using red paint, because she thinks it's a pretty colour. Suddenly her hand slips, the hand with the paintbrush, and poor Jacko the monkey now has a big red stripe across his mouth! Silly Ellie! Luckily, Mother can wash the paint off. Jacko is very relieved. That big red stripe on his mouth looked just like a scratch.

8 April

The monkey from New York

There once was a monkey,
who lived in New York.
He always used his hands to eat,
and never knife and fork!

"Because," declared the monkey
(who was in a cheerful mood),
"I find this a much easier
way to eat my food."

9 April

A special arm

Gus Monkey has an arm in plaster. Do you know
how that happened? Gus was out cycling and didn't
look where he was going. He crashed into a tree with
a great big bang. Ow! His bicycle was broken and his
arm hurt a lot. He had to go to the monkey hospital
to see the monkey doctor. The doctor said that his
arm was broken, and put it in plaster. Plaster is white
and hard. You can't move your arm any more once it
is in plaster. That is a good thing, because then the
broken bones can grow back together again.
It's not much fun for Gus with his arm in plaster,
but everyone is allowed to write their name
or do a drawing on his plaster.
That's fun, isn't it?

73

10 April

A butterfly

Davey and Kathy Monkey are playing in the wood.
"Look, over there!" says Kathy. "What a pretty butterfly!
Shall we try to catch it?" Davey and Kathy follow the
butterfly. But each time they try to catch it, it flies away.
Kathy hides behind a tree. Here comes the butterfly.
Kathy tries to catch it. Missed again! And Kathy falls right
into a puddle. She's wet all over. The butterfly lands on a
beautiful flower. Davey creeps very quietly up to the flower.
Yes, he's got it! Davey and Kathy take the butterfly home.
They ask Mother for a jam jar. They put the butterfly
in it, and they remember to prick some holes in the lid so
that the butterfly gets enough air. Now they can look at
the butterfly properly. It is yellow and brown with
a bit of orange. It has a spot on each wing.
"I feel sorry for it," says Kathy. "It can't fly any more."
Davey and Kathy take the jam jar outside.
They take the lid off. The butterfly flies away.

74

The first swimming lesson

Ernest is at the swimming pool. He is a bit worried, because he's about to have his very first swimming lesson. Ernest is nervous of going in the water. Look, there's Mother. She's coming to give him a kiss. But what's that in her hand? "A plastic monkey," she says. "This monkey likes being in the water, and he wants to join in your swimming lesson." What fun! Ernest now has a friend to take into the water with him.

12 April

The telephone monkey

Look who's sitting by himself,
it's Tony, all alone.
This silly little monkey
is always on the phone.

He rings up in the morning,
he rings by night and day.
Sometimes you'd think he'd take a
    break,
not Tony! No! No way!

He rings his mother, father, aunts,
his cousins, one, two, three.
A tele-monkey he's become,
quite silly, you'll agree.

13 April

Nicky is sad

Nicky is sad. Floppy, his pet rabbit, has died.
When animals are very old, they die. Floppy
was very old. Nicky creeps into a corner with
his cuddly monkey.
He's having a little cry about Floppy.
He stops when he notices that poor
monkey is wet through with tears.
This makes him laugh again.

14 April

What a day!

When Bert gets up in the morning, everything
starts to go wrong. When he gets out of bed,
he tries to put his slippers on, but he can't find
them. In the bathroom he slips in a puddle of
water, and catches his pyjamas on a nail on the
landing. That makes a big tear in his pyjama
trousers. And that's not all. When Bert opens
a cupboard in the kitchen to get a cup, the
cup jumps out at him. It crashes to the floor
and breaks into a thousand pieces.
"Do you know what I'm going to do?" says Bert.
"I'm going to go back to bed with my monkey.
Nothing else can go wrong then!"
So Bert does just that.

15 April

A monkey joke

Grandpa is telling Tim a story. "There is a very big tree in the wood. When spring comes, lots of little buds appear on the tree. In the summer, little tails grow out of the buds. Then, after a few good showers of rain, the little tails turn into baby monkeys. In autumn, when the monkeys are ripe, they fall gently to the ground. Then you have a whole troop of new monkeys." Tim looks at Grandpa with amazement. "Is that really true?" he asks. "Yes," replies Grandpa with a smile, "absolutely true!" Tim doesn't quite believe Grandpa's story. Would there really be a big tree in the wood that grows baby monkeys? What do you think?

16 April

The cut finger

Once there was a monkey,
who lived deep in the wood.
One day he cut his finger,
and out came drops of blood.

It only bled a little,
but it hurt a little, too.
Some sticking plaster stopped the blood,
but not the hurt, boo hoo!

His mother kissed the finger,
and said: "There there, there there,"
and now the finger's better,
"No more fussing," I declare.

The monkey clock

Benny is in the sitting room, looking at the clock. It isn't just an ordinary clock. No, it's a monkey clock with a monkey in it. There is a little door in the clock where the monkey pops out. Look, the door is opening. The monkey is coming out. "Three o'clock!" says the monkey. Benny likes looking at the clock. He likes looking at it so much that he sits and waits for a whole hour. The little door opens again. "Four o'clock!" says the monkey. What a fun clock!

18 April

Frightened of the dark

"Have you ever been afraid of the dark?" Freddy asks Rudy. "Yes, I used to be," says Rudy, "especially when it was time for bed."
"Just like me," says Freddy. "It gets so dark that you can hardly see anything at all."
"Do you know what you must do?" Rudy asks Freddy. "Take your cuddly monkey to bed with you. You won't be frightened any more, because he will look after you while you are asleep. It really does help!"

19 April

Ruth the monkey

Have you ever heard
of a monkey called Ruth?
Well, this little monkey
had a poorly tooth.
She went to the dentist,
who said: "Open wide,
I'm just going to make things
much better inside."
She felt not a thing
when he pulled out the tooth,
so now there's a happier,
gappier Ruth.

20 April

Four years old

"Oh look at that nice little insect," says Tim Monkey.
"That is a ladybird," says Grandpa. "Can you see the spots
on its back?" Tim nods his head. "Well," says Grandpa,
"some people say that if you count the number of spots on a
ladybird's back, that's how many years old it is." Tim begins
to count: "One, two, three, four. It's four years old!"
"Correct," says Grandpa. "Isn't that funny!" says Tim.
"I'm four years old, too, but I haven't
any spots on my back."
"Yes," laughs Grandpa,
"but you're a monkey,
not a ladybird!"

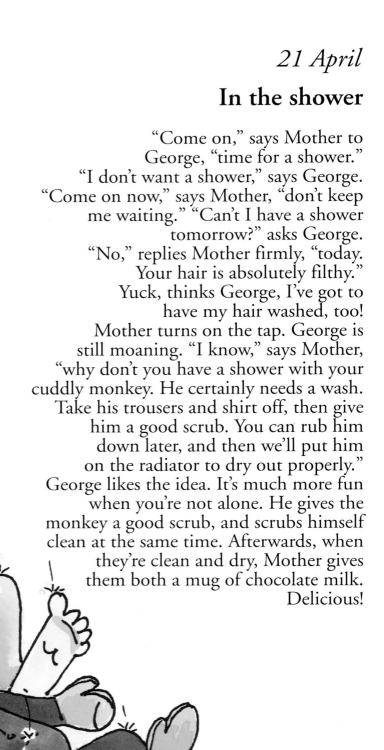

21 April

In the shower

"Come on," says Mother to George, "time for a shower."
"I don't want a shower," says George.
"Come on now," says Mother, "don't keep me waiting." "Can't I have a shower tomorrow?" asks George.
"No," replies Mother firmly, "today. Your hair is absolutely filthy."
Yuck, thinks George, I've got to have my hair washed, too!
Mother turns on the tap. George is still moaning. "I know," says Mother, "why don't you have a shower with your cuddly monkey. He certainly needs a wash. Take his trousers and shirt off, then give him a good scrub. You can rub him down later, and then we'll put him on the radiator to dry out properly."
George likes the idea. It's much more fun when you're not alone. He gives the monkey a good scrub, and scrubs himself clean at the same time. Afterwards, when they're clean and dry, Mother gives them both a mug of chocolate milk. Delicious!

22 April

On the swing together

Maria is playing in the garden. She's on the swing, going higher, and higher. All of a sudden she decides that it's no fun any more. There's nobody to talk to. Her best friend has gone shopping with her mother, and the boy next door isn't home. Wait a minute, she suddenly remembers Jacko, her monkey. She goes and fetches him. She sits him on her lap and carries on swinging. Yes, it's much more fun when there are two of you!

23 April

A monkey on the moon

There once was a monkey,
who went to the moon.
He went in a rocket.
He'll come back soon.

He built a fine house,
and had lots of fun,
watching the world,
enjoying the sun.

If you should ever
look up at the moon,
shout up to the monkey:
"Please come back soon!"

24 April

Annie Monkey goes shopping

Annie Monkey is going shopping. She's going to the baker's. Annie is carrying a very big shopping bag. Her mother has given her a shopping list. Annie needs to buy a loaf of bread, four currant buns, and a banana cake. Annie can't read yet, but she still manages to buy the things mother has written down. Do you know how she does it? She shows the shopping list to the baker. Isn't she clever?
"Good morning," says Annie when she goes into the baker's.
"Hello, Annie," says the baker. "Have you brought your shopping list?"
"Yes, I have. Here it is," says Annie, and gives the list to the baker.
The baker reads what Mother has written: "One loaf, four currant buns, and a banana cake." The baker puts the shopping in Annie's shopping bag.
Annie gives him the right money. "Goodbye, and thank you very much," she says.
"Goodbye, Annie," says the baker. "See you next time!"

25 April

The talking parrot

Two monkeys in the wood are looking at a large, brightly coloured bird. It is a parrot. The monkeys think the bird is very beautiful, but they're a bit frightened of it, too. Do you know why? Because it can talk! "I used to live in a zoo," it says, "where I learned humans' language. I am a very clever parrot, the cleverest in all the wood." The two monkeys look at each other. The bird may be beautiful and clever, but it's also very boastful!

26 April

The mud fight

Millie and Micky Monkey are playing in the wood. There are big, muddy puddles everywhere. Millie and Micky play in the mud. "Cooee," says Micky. Millie looks round and Micky throws a handful of mud on her coat. "I can do that, too," says Millie, and throws a big handful of mud at Micky. It lands right in Micky's face. Millie has to laugh. "Yeeuch," says Micky, "I'm fed up with this game." They go home together. Mother is horrified when she sees them. "What have you two been doing this time? What a filthy pair you are! Right, straight into the bath both of you, and don't forget to put your clothes in the washing basket!" Mother is a bit cross. But Millie and Micky don't really mind. The mud fight was worth it.

27 April

A hundred teapots

I know of a monkey,
who lives by herself,
with a hundred fine teapots
all on a high shelf.

Big ones and small ones,
middle-sized, too,
all coloured like jewels,
red, yellow, and blue.

Why so many teapots?
Pray, do not ask me!
Miss Monkey will tell you:
"I love to drink tea!"

28 April

Shut in

Davey has done something silly. He crept into the cupboard with his cuddly monkey and closed the door behind him. He does this sometimes when he wants a nice, quiet place to sit. But this time the door has clicked shut, and Davey can't get out. Well, he'll just have to wait until Mother finds him. But then Davey drops off to sleep … Mother looks everywhere for him, but doesn't find him for hours. Davey and his monkey are sleeping peacefully in the cupboard. When Mother wakes him up, Davey says: "It's so comfy here, may we sleep for a little longer?" Isn't Davey funny? Would you want to sleep in a cupboard?

29 April

The giraffe

"Hey, look at that," says Simon Monkey to Frank Monkey. "There's a giraffe. Why do giraffes have such long necks?" "So that they can reach the leaves in the trees," says Frank.
"Do you know what I would like to do?" says Simon. "I'd like to slide down his neck. I'm going to ask him if I may."
"Oh yes, be my guest," says the giraffe, "as long as you're careful."
Simon and Frank climb up the giraffe's neck. Simon goes first. Whoosh! He slides down very fast. It's just like a real slide. Then it's Frank's turn. Whoosh!
"That was fun," says Simon.
"Goodbye, giraffe," say Simon and Frank together. "See you tomorrow. We'll be back again."

30 April

The monkey queen's birthday

It is a special day in the monkey wood, because it is the monkey queen's birthday. All the monkeys in the wood like their queen very much. And because it is her birthday today, it is a holiday for everybody. The grown-up monkeys don't have to go to work and the little monkeys have the day off school. Everyone is celebrating. The flags are out everywhere you look. Some monkeys have even decorated their houses, and there are streamers and bunting in the trees. Everything looks very festive. All the monkeys celebrate until late in the night. Well, not every day is the monkey queen's birthday, now, is it?

1 May

May again!

There once was a monkey,
and he did say:
"I'm so very happy,
it's the month of May!

"Everything starts
to grow in May.
Plants and flowers,
lambs at play.

"The sun shines bright
all through the day.
My favourite month
is the month of May."

2 May

A boat on a string

Jon and Gary Monkey are playing down by the lake. Jon and Gary have made a boat. It is an excellent boat, made from a coconut shell. The sail is an old handkerchief. They're going to sail it now. If they blow the sail very hard, the boat sails forward all by itself. It starts off slowly, then gets faster and faster. Once it gets to the middle of the lake, the boat stops.
"Next time we make a boat, we must tie a long piece of string to it. We must fasten one end of this string to a tree, so that we can always haul it in. We're going to have to swim this time." So they do. When they get out of the water, dripping wet, the first thing they do is go in search of a long piece of string.

86

3 May

One wet foot

Esther is helping her mother clean the windows. They have got a very big bucket of water and two sponges: a large sponge and a small sponge. The large sponge is for Mother and the small sponge is for Esther. They dip the sponges in the water and then wash the window with them. Everything is starting to look very clean and bright. But what's this? Esther isn't looking at what she's doing. She's trying very hard and is concentrating on the windows. She doesn't notice where the bucket is. She steps backwards and … Splosh! She steps right into the bucket. Yuck, she's got a horrible wet foot. "Did you want to wash your foot?" laughs her mother. Esther shakes her head. "Come here then," says Mother, "let's go and find a dry sock for you. We'll carry on with the windows later." So that's what they do.

4 May

The monkey from Dingly-Dell

Have you heard of the monkey
from Dingly-Dell?
He's the monkey that likes
to ring the bell.

He climbs up the rope
(he's clever, you know)
as quick as a wink.
Then he swings to and fro.

And everyone says
at the sound of the bell:
"That must be the monkey
from Dingly-Dell."

5 May

The telephone

Otto is in the sitting room. He's a bit bored. "Mother, may I telephone my monkey?" he asks. "Yes, of course," says Mother, "I'm sure he'd like that." Otto dials a number and holds the telephone to his ear. A strange lady begins to talk to him. "Hello, Mrs Jones speaking," she says. "But I don't want to talk to you," says Otto, "I was telephoning my toy monkey, not Mrs Jones!" The lady laughs. "Oh," she says, "then you've got the wrong number. You need the monkey telephone. Goodbye, sonny!" Otto goes to find his monkey. Telephoning him is no good. He hasn't got a monkey telephone!

6 May

To the circus

There is a great big tent in town. It is a circus tent. A real circus has come to town. There are elephants and tigers, lions, acrobats, clowns, and lots more. Nick's father is taking him to the circus. They buy a ticket, then they go inside. There are seats everywhere in the big tent. (Circus people call it the big top.) Nick and his father look for good seats, so that they will be able to see everything. The show begins. A clown comes on first. The clown keeps tripping over his own shoes. Everybody laughs at him. Then it's the elephants' turn. They dance in time to music and do all sorts of tricks. Nick thinks the lions and tigers are very exciting. They're really just like cats, but much bigger and more dangerous. After the big cats come the acrobats. They do some very difficult tricks indeed. They all climb on top of each other, making a high tower of people. And they don't fall over! But Nick likes the monkeys best of all. They can do lots of tricks and they laugh at the children. When they have finished, they even clap themselves! Nick is sorry when the circus is over. But perhaps it will come again next year. Nick will be sure to go if it does!

7 May

The toy train

Alexander and Carl are playing with the toy train. It is a beautiful train. It has one engine and four carriages. The train tracks go all over the room. They sit all their cuddly toys in the train. The train takes the toys round and round the room. They go from Alexander to Carl, and then from Carl to Alexander. Oh dear, one of the toys has fallen out of the train. An accident! Carl gets the fire engine. "Toot toot, here I come," cries Alexander. "An accident! Monkey overboard!" The monkey hasn't hurt himself, and is soon back in the train. And he continues happily on his journey.

8 May

The smelly monkey

There once was a monkey
who said: "Golly gosh!
I've decided: in future
I shan't ever wash!"

He had dirty ears,
dirty hands, dirty feet –
the dirtiest monkey
you ever could meet.

When he asked: "What is wrong?
Why no friends? Please do tell."
Folk said: "Have a good wash,
'cos you're starting to smell!"

9 May

A nest in the tree

Hunky and Thomas Monkey are playing in the wood. "Look up there," says Hunky. "There's something moving in that tree." Thomas looks at the tree. "That's a bird," says Thomas. "The bird has built a nest in the tree. Shall we have a look to see if there's anything in it?" The two monkeys climb up the tree. "We must be very quiet," says Thomas, "otherwise we will frighten the bird." They sit on a branch close to the nest. They have a good view of the nest from where they are sitting. "The bird is sitting on the eggs," says Thomas. "She has laid her eggs in the nest, and they need to be kept warm. So she is sitting on them. She'll sit on them until they're ready to hatch. That's when the baby birds come out of the eggs." The bird flies off. "Look," says Hunky, "there are four eggs in the nest." "Yes," says Thomas, "so when they're ready to hatch, four baby birds will come out of them. It will take a little while, though. We'll come back in a few days and look to see if the eggs have hatched." Hunky thinks that's a good idea. So they climb down the tree.

10 May

Mother's birthday

It is Maria's mother's birthday today. Maria has bought a lovely present for her mother with her own money. Very early in the morning, when it's still dark, she goes into Mother's bedroom and announces: "A present for your birthday!" Mother wakes up with a start. Maria gives her a present, all nicely wrapped up, which Mother unwraps straight away. Inside is a lovely little cuddly monkey.

"I've got a cuddly monkey, but you didn't have any cuddly toys, and that wasn't fair," says Maria. "So I bought you one," she adds proudly.

Mother thinks the monkey is very beautiful and gives Maria a big kiss to say thank you very much.

11 May

German measles

Stephen doesn't feel very well when he wakes up in the morning. Do you think he might be ill? He gets out of bed and goes to the bathroom. He looks at himself in the mirror. Oh no! His face is covered in red spots. Stephen looks down at his arms. They're covered in red spots, too. So are his legs, his feet, and his tummy! "Oh dear," says his mother, "you've got German measles. It won't last long, but you will have to stay in bed." So Stephen goes back to bed with all his cuddly toys. He doesn't mind a bit. He quite likes the idea of a day in bed with German measles.

12 May

The lion tamer

There once was a monkey,
who lived in Cramer.
He said: "I will be
a lion tamer."

He bought a big whip,
and a very big cage,
a chair, a new suit,
so he looked all the rage.

He'd all that he needed,
except the big cat,
he searched everywhere
(even under his hat).

But nowhere could he find one,
that monkey from Cramer,
so he stayed as he was,
and not a lion tamer.

So, if you are a lion,
and you don't know what to do,
just call upon our monkey friend,
he has a plan for you!

13 May

Flowers in the garden

Janey is in the garden. She is looking at the flowers. Janey planted the bulbs herself in the autumn. After winter had passed, the bulbs began to grow roots, then later green shoots appeared. The green shoots have turned into leaves and stems with flowers on them. They are called daffodils. There are a lot of them. The garden is full of daffodils. Janey sits her cuddly monkey down among the daffodils.
What a lovely place to sit, he thinks.

14 May

An angry neighbour

"Are you coming to play football?"
Danny asks his friend William. Danny
and William go out into the garden with
the ball. "Look out, here it comes!"
says William, and kicks the ball to Danny.
"I can kick much harder than that!"
says Danny. "Watch me." So Danny gives
the ball a really hard kick. Oh dear,
the ball crashes through the neighbour's
window. The window is broken and
the neighbour is cross.
"You young whipper-snappers, you!"
he says angrily. "Go and kick your ball
somewhere else and leave my windows
alone!" Danny and William beat
a hasty retreat.

15 May

A rainbow

Olly and Polly Monkey are out for a walk in the wood.
It has just stopped raining, and now the sun has
come out. "Oh look, up there in the sky," says Olly.
"A rainbow. The sun does that. The sun shines against
the rain. Look. It's still raining over there and the sun
is shining here. The sun is shining against the rain
over there and that makes a rainbow."
"Oh," says Polly, "I'm not sure I completely
understand. But it does look lovely. Don't you agree?"
Olly nods, he thinks the rainbow
is beautiful, too.

95

16 May

Alexander Monkey

I know a monkey
who laughs all day.
He's called Alexander
and loves to play.

He laughs and laughs,
and down his face
run tears of laughter
as if they're in a race.

So much laughter
makes his eyes go red.
So now Alexander
goes off to his bed.

17 May

In the lift

Mark is going with his mother to visit Grandma. Mark's cuddly monkey is going, too. Grandma lives in a flat. There are lots of other flats in the building. Grandma lives high up, on the sixth floor. Mark and his mother go in the lift. Mark likes the lift much better than the stairs. Mark and his monkey may press the button. Bzzz, here is the lift. It takes them gently up to the sixth floor. Grandma is already waiting for them. "How lovely to see you," she says. "There's tea for Mother, and lemonade for Mark and Monkey. Come inside."

18 May

The old photograph

Paula is looking at a photograph in a frame. "Mother," asks Paula, "who are these people in this photograph?" "That's a very old photograph," says Mother.
"But who are they?" says Paula. It is a photograph of two children who each have a cuddly monkey on their knee. "One of them is me," says Mother, "and the other is Aunt Lucy. It was taken a long time ago. I was the same age as you are now. Just think of that!" Paula especially likes the two cuddly monkeys.

19 May

Mowing a monkey

Martin is in the garden with Father. They are mowing the grass. Father is pushing the lawnmower. The lawnmower is cutting the grass nice and short. "May I have a go?" asks Martin. Martin puts his cuddly monkey down on the grass and begins to push the lawnmower. It's very difficult, and the lawnmower goes the wrong way. Martin mows right over his monkey! The monkey was very lucky not to be hurt.
"Hey, Martin," says Father, "you're supposed to be mowing the grass, not mowing a monkey!"

20 May

The monkey with the banana

A monkey peeled a banana,
something he loved to eat.
He didn't think –
and dropped the skin.
It fell close by his feet.

And, seeking more bananas,
(the really yummy kind),
he put his foot upon that skin,
and fell on his behind!

21 May

The eggs hatch

Hunky and Thomas Monkey are up a tree.
They are looking at birds' eggs in a nest.
"Look," says Hunky, "one of them is moving."
A hole appears in the egg. Out of the hole
appears a tiny beak. The hole gets bigger.
A tiny head pokes out of the hole. Soon the
whole baby bird appears. Not just one egg
hatches, but all of them. Mother bird arrives.
Her beak is full of worms. She stuffs a worm
in each tiny, hungry beak. "Yuck," says Hunky.
"Worms, I hate worms."
Thomas just laughs. "But you're not a bird,"
he says.
"I'm very glad I'm not a bird," says Hunky.
"I much prefer bananas!"

22 May

The hall of mirrors

Molly is at the fair with her mother and her cuddly monkey. Molly is holding her monkey tight so that she doesn't lose him. There's lots to do at the fair. There is a merry-go-round, bumper-cars, and a ghost-train. Next to the ghost-train is a hall of mirrors. Very strange mirrors. When Molly stands in front of one of them, it makes her look very tall and thin. Monkey looks very tall and thin, too. "Look, Mother," says Molly, "don't we look funny!" Another mirror makes her monkey look short and fat. Molly laughs at him. She likes this much better than the bumper-cars.

23 May

The monkey from Timbuktu

Once there was a monkey,
who lived in Timbuktu.
He asked the strangest questions,
like "why?" and "where?" and "who?"
"Why is the earth round like a ball?
why is there left and right?
Why does the moon sleep all day long
and stay awake all night?
Where is my shadow hiding,
when I'm in bed asleep?
Where do my footsteps go to,
when up the stairs I creep?"
Everyone just walked away
and left him on his own.
The answers he will never get,
he now lives all alone.

Feeding the ducks

Will and Madeleine Monkey are playing by the lake in the wood. They have brought a large bag of stale bread with them. They're going to feed the ducks. They feed the ducks quite often. But it will be even more fun today, because there are ducklings, too. Will and Madeleine throw some bits of bread in the water. The ducks swim over quickly. There is one very big duck among them. Each time a small duck tries to get a piece of bread, the big duck chases it away. Will thinks it's not fair. He tries to chase the big duck away. "Shoo, shoo!" he shouts, but it doesn't help. Will goes closer to the edge of the lake. "Hey, big duck, go away!" he shouts and waves his arms. "Look out!" cries Madeleine, but it's too late. Will falls in the lake with a great big splash. He is lucky that the lake is not very deep. But he is dripping wet and covered in duckweed. It looks as if he's wearing a silly hat. Will clambers out of the water. "You're wet all over," says Madeleine, "but it was worth it. That big duck got such a fright that he swam off as fast as he could. Now the little ducks can eat their bread in peace."

25 May

Playing school

Jenny is playing school. All her dolls and cuddly toys are sitting in a row.
Jenny is the teacher and she tells the children to be quiet. "Chatty Monkey,
stop talking!" she says sternly. But Chatty just keeps on talking.
"Chatty," says Jenny, "if you keep on talking, you'll never learn how to write nicely.
You'll just stay a silly little monkey. You must pay attention."
But Chatty doesn't want to learn to write. He likes chatting to the dolls much better.
"Go and stand in the corner," says Jenny bossily. "There's no-one to talk to there!"
Poor Chatty, standing there in the corner. Well, he shouldn't have been chatting
with the dolls, should he?

26 May

Banana bellies!

Davey and Harry Monkey are in the wood. They are picking bananas. The tree is full of bananas. Davey and Harry throw the bananas down from the tree. Underneath it there is already a great big pile of bananas. When they have picked all the bananas, they climb down. "We had better try the bananas," says Harry, "before we take them home." "I agree," says Davey. Davey and Harry sit down, lean their backs against the tree, and each take a banana. They peel them, take a bite, and Davey says: "Mmm, what delicious bananas!" "Yes," says Harry, "I could sit here and eat bananas all day." They each take another banana. And another, and another, until they must have eaten twenty bananas each. Their tummies are almost hurting. They lie back against the tree. "Gosh, my tummy's got really fat!" says Davey. "So's mine," says Harry. "We've got banana bellies!" They fall about laughing. They're so full that they fall asleep under the tree.

The carpenter monkey

Francis Monkey is helping his father in the shed. Francis's father is a carpenter monkey. He makes things from wood. He can make cupboards, or tables, or even a rabbit hutch. He has a saw and a hammer. He knocks nails in the wood with his hammer. And with a pair of pincers he can pull them out again. He can make almost anything. Francis's father is making a rabbit hutch today. Francis is helping his father. Francis is allowed to knock in the nails with the hammer. He has to concentrate very hard when he is helping his father. Francis would like to be a carpenter monkey, too, when he grows up.

28 May

The cold monkey

A cold little monkey
took paper and wood.
He made a warm fire
and then he felt good.
He warmed his front,
and he warmed his back.
The fire then started
to spark and crack.
He thought that the fire
was getting too hot.
"Ouch, ouch!" he cried,
"I've burnt my bot!"

103

29 May

The made-up monkey

Milly and Tanya are in their mother's bedroom. Mother has some lipstick and eyeshadow on a shelf, and some other interesting things, too. What fun! They decide to put some make-up on their cuddly monkey. They give him red lips using the lipstick and black eyelashes with lots of the mascara. Then they add some eyeshadow. Finally, they put lots of rouge on his cheeks. When they have finished, Milly and Tanya start to laugh. Their monkey looks a bit like a clown! Milly finds a necklace and a red bow in a box. Doesn't the monkey look smart wearing them?

30 May

A puncture

Tim is cycling on his new, red bicycle with his cuddly monkey on the back. But oh no! There's a nail right in his path and Tim hasn't seen it. He rides right over the nail. "Pssssssst," goes his front tyre. A puncture. Tim gets off his bike and walks home. When he gets home, he tells his father what has happened. Father says he will mend the tyre so that Tim and his monkey can go out cycling again. But do look where you're going next time, Tim!

31 May

Micky's sticky hands

Micky and Millie Monkey are sitting at the kitchen table. They are glueing things. They cut shapes out of coloured paper with a pair of scissors, then stick them onto white paper. Millie is making a flower and Micky is making a house. Micky's house is almost finished. He's just got the roof to do.
"The roof must be red," says Micky. He reaches out for the scissors. But oh dear, his hands stick to the scissors.
"What are you doing?" asks Millie. "I forgot that I had glue on my hands. Now I'm stuck to the scissors," says Micky. Millie bursts out laughing. Micky looks so funny with the scissors stuck to his hand. There is paper stuck to him, too.
Mother comes into the room. She laughs, too.
"I think I'll leave you like that," she says, "then you won't be able to get up to any more mischief."
Micky doesn't think it's a bit funny. "Come on then," says Mother. "Let's go and unstick you, my little sticky Micky!"

105

1 June

The monkey who loves to read

I know a monkey
called Double Dutch,
who loves to read,
very, very much!

Whether he's with friends
or fishing in a brook,
he's always got
his nose in a book.

It doesn't matter
where you look,
you'll always see him,
his nose in a book.

2 June

The beautiful necklace

Annette is playing in the garden. She is making a necklace. Not just an
ordinary necklace, but a necklace made of daisies. Daisies are small,
white flowers with yellow middles that you find growing in the grass.
Annette has picked lots of daisies. They are lying on the grass next to her.
Annette picks up a daisy. She makes a slit in the stem, near the bottom.
She sticks the stem of a second daisy through this slit. And in the stem of
the second daisy she makes another slit, through which she sticks a third
daisy. And so on, and so on. When the necklace is finished, she puts it
round her cuddly monkey's neck. It looks beautiful.

3 June

A fibber

Jacob Monkey is almost always good. But sometimes he can be a bit naughty. Sometimes he tells fibs. Fibbing is saying something that's not true. When Jacob had secretly been sneaking biscuits from the biscuit tin, Mother asked him if he had been eating the biscuits. "No, not me," said Jacob. But it was him. If you have done something, you must say that you have done it. Mother found out, of course, that Jacob had eaten the biscuits. "Sometimes you're a real little fibber," she said to Jacob. Jacob had to promise that he would never tell fibs again. Do you think he will keep his promise?

4 June

A prickly rose

Hunky and Thomas Monkey are playing in the garden.
"Look," says Hunky, "aren't these beautiful flowers?"
"Those are red roses," says Thomas. "I'm going to pick them for my mother."
He bends over to pick a rose. "Be careful!" calls out Hunky, but it is too late.
"Ouch," says Thomas, "that rose pricked my finger!"
"Silly monkey," says Hunky, "don't you know that roses have prickles?" Thomas looks at his finger. It doesn't hurt much. It's nearly better. "I think I'll leave the rose alone," he says. "I'll pick a different flower for my mother. One that doesn't prick!"

5 June

The giant monkey

Can you see the monkey
with the great long legs?
With the big, big feet
and the long, long toes?

Can you see the monkey
with the great big tummy?
With the long, long hands
and a mouth that's funny?

With a head so large,
and arms as long as that,
if that's not a giant,
then I'll eat my hat!

6 June

Building a house

Mary Louise is building a house from blocks.
She has a very big box of lots of different sorts
of blocks. Mary Louise builds the walls first.
The walls must be strong, otherwise the house
will fall down. Then comes the roof. She also
gives the house a door and a window.
There, the house is finished. It is a beautiful
house. Mary Louise would like to live in it,
but that wouldn't be possible. It's far too small.
Jake the toy monkey may live in it instead.
It's just his size. So it really should be
called a monkey house.

The blue swimming hat

Will loves going swimming. He is a very good swimmer. He has already got two swimming certificates. When you go swimming, you get wet. Your hair gets wet, too. And Will just hates getting his hair wet. Will has solved the problem. When he goes swimming, he puts his swimming hat on. It isn't a hat to keep your head warm, it's a hat to keep your hair dry. When Will goes swimming, he puts his swimming trunks on first, and then his swimming hat. His hat is blue. Will takes his cuddly monkey swimming. He has a swimming hat, too, but he refuses to wear it. It would be a better idea if Will took his plastic duck with him to the swimming pool. Then the monkey can sit and watch from the side, nice and dry.

8 June

A calf

Jon lives on a farm where there are a lot of animals. There are cows and sheep, chickens, and sometimes horses. Jon really likes living on a farm, especially today. A calf was born today. A calf is a baby cow. The calf is standing next to its mother, drinking her milk. This will make the calf grow big and strong. When it is fully grown, the calf will be a cow. Jon holds his cuddly monkey tight and puts his thumb in his mouth. I'm glad you won't grow up to be a great big monkey, he thinks, because then you wouldn't fit in my bed with me any more.

9 June

The monkey from Jeddah

There once was a monkey,
who lived in Jeddah,
and the trousers he wore,
well, they seemed to get redder.

And then his red sweater
got brighter as well.
You'd think that those garments
were under a spell.

So the monkey from Jeddah,
in the red clothes he wore,
could be seen from afar.
He was hard to ignore!

10 June

The caterpillar parcel

Theo Monkey has found something funny. It looks a bit like a bean, but it isn't. He shows it to his mother when he gets home. "Mother, look what I've found," says Theo.
"Oh," says mother, "that's a cocoon. A cocoon is a caterpillar wrapped up in a parcel."
"A caterpillar wrapped up in a parcel?" asks Theo.
He doesn't understand.
"Yes," says Mother, "a caterpillar parcel. Once a caterpillar has eaten enough food and grown big enough, it wraps itself up. That is called a cocoon. If you wait a while, the cocoon will open. And out will come a butterfly."
"Really?" asks Theo.
"Really and truly," says Mother. "I know. Let's put the cocoon in a jam jar. Then you can keep it, and when it's time, you can see the butterfly coming out."
Theo goes and fetches a jam jar. He puts the cocoon in it. He's not sure if he should believe his mother or not. It sounds such a strange story. But it might be true. What do you think?

11 June

The sunflower

It is a lovely day, so Tim is sitting in the garden
with Grandpa and his cuddly monkey.
"Grandpa," says Tim, "may I ask you a question?"
"Of course," says Grandpa.
"You see that big flower over there?" says Tim,
"the very tall one, with the long stem and
yellow petals. What is it called?"
"That is a sunflower," answers Grandpa.
"A sunflower? Why is it called a sunflower?" asks Tim.
"It's called a sunflower because it looks like the sun,"
says Grandpa. "Look, the yellow petals look just
like sunbeams."
"Perhaps," says Tim, "but the sun hasn't got a stalk,
has it? And the flower has. Is my cuddly monkey a
sunmonkey, because he's got a yellow jacket and
that looks like the sun?"
Grandpa laughs. A sunmonkey!
What ever will Tim think of next!

12 June

A monkey out walking

"Hello there, Mr Monkey,
walking down the street.
Would you like to tell us
who you're going to meet?"
"Nobody special," he said,
pulling up a sock.
"I just felt it would be nice
to walk around the block."

13 June

The monkey princess

Jenny and Martin are playing up in
the attic with the dressing-up clothes.
The dolls and the cuddly monkey are
there, too. Jenny dresses them all up
beautifully. Martin is the king and
Jenny is the queen. Monkey is the
princess and the dolls are just ordinary
people. "I am the king," says Martin,
"so you must all do as I say."
"And I'm the queen and you must do
as I say, too," says Jenny, "except
Monkey, because she is the princess."
Monkey doesn't say anything.
She has fallen asleep.

14 June

A monkey puzzle

Gemma is doing a jigsaw puzzle with lots of small pieces. She has the picture of the puzzle next to her. She can find where the pieces go by looking at the picture. It is a jigsaw puzzle of a monkey. Gemma has already done the monkey's face. Now she's looking for the pieces with his hands on them. When Gemma picks up a piece, she looks at the picture to find where it must go. She has nearly finished the puzzle. One more piece to go. That's not so difficult. There's only one hole left over!

15 June

Davey Monkey

Do you know a monkey called Davey?
He'll stay in his bed all the day.
And if you find him something to do,
just listen to what he will say:

"I don't want to get my hands dirty.
Work is frightfully messy," he said.
"And if I get up, I'll get tired again,
so I might as well stay in my bed."

16 June

Shaving

Tom is in the bathroom with Father. Tom has just got washed and Father is shaving. First he puts shaving foam on his face. That looks really funny. His cheeks are all white with foam. Then he takes a razor and shaves it all off. You have to be very careful with razors, because they are very sharp.

"Father, why do you have to shave?" asks Tom.

"Well, if I don't shave," says Father, "I'll grow a long beard, and I don't want to. So I shave the hairs off."

"But I don't shave," says Tom, "and I haven't got a long beard, have I?"

"No," says Father with a laugh, "you only start to grow a beard when you are older."

"Why do you only grow a beard?" asks Tom. "Monkeys have hair everywhere. Why haven't we? And why don't monkeys shave?"

Father laughs again. He can just imagine it: a great big monkey with a razor!

17 June

The baby birds leave the nest

Hunky and Thomas Monkey are looking at a nest in the tree. At first there were four eggs in the nest. Four baby birds came out of them. The baby birds have now grown into bigger birds. They have eaten lots of worms. All the worms have made them grow big and strong. Now they have to learn to fly. The mother bird pushes the babies to the edge of the nest. Then she gives them another little push. The big baby birds fall out of the nest and begin to fly. Just like that! That's something monkeys can't do, can they?

18 June

Michael is cross

Michael is cross because his sister Sonya has broken his toy monkey. Sonya was playing with the monkey and now his ear is torn. "Why are you looking so cross?" Mother asks Michael. "I'm cross with Sonya," says Michael. "She broke my monkey." "I know what to do," says Mother, "give the monkey to me. I'll mend his ear." The monkey is mended in no time. "You're not cross any more?" asks Mother. No, Michael has stopped being cross, because his monkey is mended

117

19 June

Sleeping monkeys

Somewhere in the great big wood,
there stands a big, tall tree.
The tree is full of monkeys,
it's the sleeping tree, you see.

All night long they dream
of other monkeys far away.
Friends in distant lands
awake where it is day.

So they dream all night,
snuggled close and warm.
The sleeping tree keeps them
safe from any harm.

20 June

Father's Day

Edward has done a lovely drawing at school.
He has drawn a father monkey with a house and two
trees. Do you know why? It is nearly Father's Day.
On Father's Day, fathers are given presents and special
treats all day long. Edward's drawing is his Father's
Day present. The teacher rolls up his drawing
very carefully. Then she ties a big bow around it.
The present is ready. Edward takes the drawing
home and hides it under his bed. Father is not
allowed to see the drawing until Father's Day.

21 June

Summer begins

Summer begins today. The sun shines a lot in the summer. Then it is nice and warm outside. It's warm in the monkey wood, too. The monkeys are all very happy when summer comes. Then they can play outside in the trees, because the weather is so good. Edward is also happy that it is summer. That means he can go to the beach, where he can go swimming, build sand castles, and look for shells. Edward can go to the wood, too. Perhaps he will meet a monkey there. What do you think?

22 June

A new tooth

Frank is getting a new tooth. His old, milk tooth started to get wobbly and then fell out. There was a hole in the place where the tooth used to be. Now a new tooth is growing in this hole. Frank looks in the mirror every day and sees the tooth getting bigger and bigger. Mother sees it, too. "When you get a new tooth," she says, "you get a present, too. Look." Mother gives Frank a new toothbrush with a monkey on it. What fun! Frank wouldn't mind getting a new tooth every day!

23 June

Nell the monkey

Listen here,
while I tell
about a monkey
they call Nell.

Nell is good at knitting,
with wool, and needles (two).
She makes socks for the monkeys,
coloured purple, pink, and blue.

If you should see a monkey
in knitted socks, do tell.
I'm sure that they were knitted
by that clever monkey, Nell.

24 June

New wallpaper

Maria has new wallpaper in her bedroom. It looks beautiful. It has monkeys on it.
Monkeys sitting on swings, monkeys swimming, and monkeys climbing trees.
There must be a thousand monkeys in Maria's bedroom. It's so lovely, thinks Maria.
Now I'll never be by myself any more, because I'll always have my monkeys.
I've got lots of friends to talk to.

25 June

Plaits everywhere

Fiona Monkey has very long hair. Her hair is nearly down to her knees. Fiona usually ties it back in a ponytail. But today she would like something different. She wants plaits. That's a lot of work with such long hair. Mother helps Fiona. Fiona begins on one side and Mother on the other. There are going to be lots of plaits. Once Fiona has finished a plait, she ties a bow at the end. She uses lots of different coloured ribbons. She has already done a red one, a green one, a blue one, and a yellow one. The plaits look very colourful. I've never seen anyone with so many plaits as Fiona Monkey.

26 June

Donald makes music

Donald and Jacky Monkey are making music. Donald bangs his drum very hard and walks around the room. Jacky is playing a trumpet. "We are a band!" cries Donald. "We're going to be famous and we'll be on the television."
Mother comes into the room. "What a lot of noise," she says. "Could you turn the sound down a bit, please? It sounds lovely, but it is very loud. It's giving me a bit of a headache." Donald bangs the drum very quietly. "We are a quiet band now," he says.

27 June

A big monkey

There once was a monkey,
who was very small,
and oh, how he wanted
to be very tall!

So he ate and he ate,
twenty times every day.
Now he's twenty times bigger
in every way.

He eats and he eats.
How I wish he would stop.
If he eats one more mouthful,
I'm sure he'll go POP!

A shower of rain?

It is very warm outside. It hasn't rained for a few days. So Tom and his toy monkey Jake are going to water the flowers in the garden. Tom has a lovely green watering-can. First he waters the roses and then the daisies. He doesn't forget the forget-me-nots, either. Father is sitting outside in a chair. He is reading a newspaper. Wait a minute, thinks Tom, I'll play a trick on Father. Quietly, he goes over to his father and pours a little water over Father's foot. The foot moves. But Father hasn't realized what is happening. So Tom pours a little more water over Father's foot. Father looks up from his newspaper. Tom quickly hides the watering-can behind his back. Father looks first at Tom and then at his foot. "I just don't understand," he says, "I'm sure I felt water on my foot. Did Jake do it, do you think?" "Oh, no," says Tom, "that was a shower of rain. A very small one." "Really?" asks Father. "Really," says Tom. Father goes back to his newspaper and Tom laughs to himself. Father thought that Jake had made his foot wet. How silly!

29 June

New shoes

Nicholas has some very nice shoes. They are new. They were bought yesterday when
Nicholas and Mother went shopping. Nicholas is allowed to wear his new shoes today.
He hardly dares walk around in them. He sits down on the sofa with his cuddly
monkey Jake and looks at his shoes. "What are you doing?" asks Mother.
"I'm looking at my shoes," answers Nicholas. "Go and play outside," says Mother.
"Your shoes are to walk around in, not just to look at."
Nicholas takes Jake outside with him. It has just been raining and there are
lots of puddles. Nicholas is a bit bored, because his friend isn't outside.
He throws Jake into the air with a swing of his arm. But oh dear, Jake lands in a puddle.
Nicholas walks on tiptoe through the puddle, but his feet still get wet. Wet like Jake.
Mother is not pleased. "You didn't have to make your brand new shoes wet the first
time you put them on!" she says. "Take them off, they need to dry out."
What a shame. Nicholas can't wear his lovely new shoes now.

30 June

An elephant shower

Boris and Vincent Monkey are out for a walk in the wood. "Gosh, isn't it warm?"
says Boris. "I don't think I've ever felt quite so hot as I do today."
"Yes, I agree," says Vincent.
Then Boris and Vincent meet an elephant.
"Hello," says the elephant, "how do you do?"
"Actually," says Boris, "we're far too hot."
"Then I have an excellent idea," says the elephant. "Come along with me."
Boris and Vincent go with the elephant to the lake in the wood. "Wait a moment,"
says the elephant and sticks his trunk in the water. He sucks up a trunkful of water
and spurts it all over the two hot monkeys. It makes them jump. "There," says the
elephant, "that was a lovely, cold, elephant shower. I bet you're not quite so hot now."
Boris and Vincent shake their heads. No, they're not so hot any more.
They're just a bit wet. But they'll dry.

125

1 July

The monkey with the scooter

A monkey with a scooter
set off to travel far.
He thought he'd go to Africa,
and call at Zanzibar.

So, one leg on and one leg off,
he whizzed off down the street.
He'd better get a move on,
for it's nearly time to eat.

And when he'd been around the world,
and back to his front door,
that monkey picked his scooter up,
and did it all once more.

2 July

Foot painting

Anna is painting with finger-paint and her hands
are covered in paint. Her cuddly monkey is sitting
next to her. He's allowed to paint, too. Anna puts
some paint on his foot and presses the foot onto the
paper. The monkey's foot makes a really good print
on the paper. When Mother comes in, the monkey
is covered in paint.
"Well," says Mother, "I think Monkey will have to go
in the washing machine. Just look at him, he's filthy!"
Oh dear, Anna hadn't thought of that!

3 July

The sun hat

Benny Monkey has a new hat. It is a very special hat, a sun hat. It has a very wide brim. This will stop the sun from shining in his eyes. Benny is very proud of his hat. He puts it on and walks around in the wood so that all his friends can see him. They don't just see the sun hat, they also see that it is a bit too big for him. So much too big, in fact, that Benny can hardly see where he's going. He has to put his hands out in front of him to feel his way. The other monkeys think Benny looks very funny and laugh at him. What a silly sun hat, they think. Excellent at keeping the sun out of your eyes, but no good at all if you want to see where you're going!

4 July

Dan's alarm clock

Every evening about seven,
Dan the monkey goes to bed.
He has a small alarm clock.
He keeps it by his bed.

But when it comes to morning,
and Dan is still in bed,
the alarm goes off (just like a bomb).
The sound would wake the dead!

5 July

Cuddly

Cuddly is enjoying himself. Cuddly is going to the beach with Jenny.
First they go on the bus, then on the train, and then they're there, at the beach.
Cuddly is Jenny's cuddly monkey. He sleeps with Jenny in her bed every night,
but he has never been to the beach before. He hopes he'll be allowed to collect
shells with Jenny. He thinks that will be fun.

6 July

Making a box

Jenny and Cuddly are sitting at the table.
They have spent the whole day at the beach.
Do you know what they did there? They looked
for shells and built a sand-castle. Jenny put all the
shells in a big bag. She brought it home with her.
Now Jenny and Cuddly are sticking shells onto
empty boxes. Yellow, and pink, and blue shells.
The boxes look very nice. But Cuddly is getting
a bit tired. He's going to bed in a minute, where
he'll fall asleep and dream of shells, and the
sand-castle …

129

7 July

Swimming

The monkeys in the big wood
are a bit bored. "What shall we do?"
asks Jamie Monkey.
"Let's go swimming," says Ricky, the smallest
monkey. He's still quite young and isn't very good
at swimming, yet. Swimming, what a good idea.
So they all go along to the swimming pool. It's very busy
there today. Lots of monkeys have decided to go swimming.
"Look," says Jamie suddenly, "there's a diving board. Let's all
jump off the diving board." They all climb up the steps and jump,
one after the other, off the diving board.
All except Ricky. "I'm scared," he says. Some monkeys are jumping
and others are swinging by their tails, but Ricky still doesn't dare.
Jamie says to Ricky: "Don't look down for too long, or you'll be even
more frightened. I'll show you. Keep your legs together and hold your
arms up in the air, then you'll land nice and straight in the water.
There's nothing to it."
Ricky looks down into the pool once more and thinks: right, here
goes. Eyes closed and … jump! He lands in the water with a big splosh!
Look at him laughing. "That was fun," he says, "let's do it again!"

8 July

Torn clothes

Tim the monkey
is very unlucky.
Accidents happen each day.
He trips over a ledge
or falls into a hedge.
He's not safe to send out to play.

His jacket is torn
(it's hardly been worn),
his trousers have got a big hole.
His shirt is in tatters
(not that this matters),
his shoes are worn through the sole.

His mother tries hard
with industrious sewing
to mend all the holes.
He puts the clothes on
and away he is gone,
and tears them all over again!

9 July

The sea in a shell

Timmy Monkey has found a shell. Timmy picks up the shell and holds it up to his ear. Hey, Timmy hears a swishing noise. What is it? It can't be the trees rustling in the wind, because it's not windy. Then Timmy has an idea: perhaps there is a tiny sea in the shell, with tiny little waves! That'll be it. What fun, Timmy has his own little sea!

10 July

A free ice-cream

Billy Monkey is playing on the beach. He's playing with a beach ball. It's one of those great big balls you have to blow up. The beach ball isn't very heavy. Oh dear, here comes a gust of wind. The wind whisks the ball away. Billy goes after it trying to catch it. But the beach ball rolls further and further away from him. Billy starts to run. He must be able to catch it! But oh dear again, Billy is looking at the ball and not where he's going. He doesn't see another monkey sitting there eating an ice-cream. Boom! Billy crashes into the monkey with a great big bang. The ice-cream flies through the air and lands upside down right on Billy's head! What a thing to happen! Luckily neither monkey has hurt himself, and the monkey who lost his ice-cream isn't cross either. Billy licks the ice-cream that is dripping down his face. Mmmm, yummy. Not a bad way to get a free ice-cream, thinks Billy.

11 July

A play

Anita Monkey has got dressing-up clothes on. Very grand ones. She looks like a very rich lady. Do you know what she's doing? Together with Frank Monkey she's doing a play. Anita and Frank are acting. They are supposed to be very important people. Frank has a costume on, too. He looks just like a very rich gentleman. Anita and Frank are putting on very refined accents when they talk. Father and Mother are watching the play. They think it's very good. At the end of the play, Anita and Frank make deep bows to the audience. They bend over forwards so far that their noses almost touch their knees. Father and Mother clap enthusiastically. They really enjoyed the play.

12 July

Always friends

There's a very tiny monkey,
who could hide in my closed hand,
and although he's oh so tiny,
he's the bravest in the land.

His elephant friend once told him
(and this is very true),
no matter if you're big or small,
be brave and you'll get through.

So whether your friends are very big,
or very, very small,
true friends will pull together –
that's the best friendship of all.

133

13 July

The garden hose

Freddy is in the garden. It is a beautiful day.
The sun is shining, and Freddy is hot. I know,
he thinks, I'll get the garden hose. I'll fill this
bucket with cold water from the hose. Then I can
put my feet in the bucket to cool down. Freddy
gets hold of the garden hose and turns the tap on.
The bucket is full of cold water in no time. When
Freddy puts his feet in the nice cold water he feels
much cooler straight away. Then he notices his
cuddly monkey lying there in the grass. He must
be hot, too. Perhaps he would like to cool his feet
in the bucket. Freddy picks up his monkey and
holds him over the bucket. But oh dear, Freddy's
hands are wet, and Monkey slips out of them.
Splosh! Monkey dives into the water.
He's dripping wet when Freddy
manages to fish him out.
But never mind, the hot sun
will dry him in no time!

14 July

Abroad

Freddy is going on holiday with Mother, Father, and his cuddly monkey Jake. They're going to another country, a long way away. It is a very long way, but they get there in the end. Freddy picks up Jake and goes outside. There are some other children. Freddy goes up to them. But what's this? These children are talking very strangely. Freddy doesn't understand what they're saying. Then Freddy remembers that they're in a different country. They speak a different language of course! Now Freddy understands. He doesn't mind at all. You can still play together, even if you don't understand each other completely. And if he gets fed up, he can always play with Jake!

15 July

Camping in the garden

"Pass me that tent pole, Tom," says Father. Tom gives the tent pole to Father. Tom is helping with the tent. Father and Tom are putting up the tent in the garden. They're going on a camping holiday in a few days. But first they have to check that the tent is in one piece. That's why they're setting up the tent in the garden. A tent has to be well anchored to the ground, otherwise it will blow away. Tom and his cuddly monkey are allowed to sleep in the tent tonight. Tom thinks it's quite exciting to camp in his own garden.

135

16 July

A monkey with one tooth

A long time ago
(when I was in my youth),
a monkey in a far off land
was born with just one tooth.

A problem you might think?
(I thought that's what you'd say.)
No problem whatsoever,
not in the slightest way.

"I don't mind having just one tooth,"
the little monkey said.
"Who needs teeth for bananas?
I simply suck instead!"

17 July

Tying your shoelaces

Do you know what Sam has learnt to do? He has learnt to tie his shoelaces. It wasn't that easy to learn. No, it was quite difficult. Father told him how to do it, then showed him by tying Sam's toy monkey's shoelaces. So Sam got a good idea of how to do it. Then he tried it himself. He kept practising on his monkey's shoelaces. As soon as he could do that, he tried it on his own shoes. And it worked. Good for you, Sam!

18 July

The sand-castle

Boris and Vincent Monkey are on the beach. They are building a castle. Not a real castle, but a sand-castle. First they make a big pile of sand. On top of the pile they make some towers, just like on a real castle. The sand-castle is very big. It has four towers. Boris and Vincent decorate the sand-castle with shells. They find the shells on the beach. There are lots of them. The sand-castle looks very good and is almost finished. It just needs a flag on top. The flag can flutter in the wind.

19 July

The sack race

Gareth and Wally Monkey are playing a lovely game. They both have a large sack. Gareth and Wally get into their sacks. Then they begin to jump. Whoever gets to the other side of the garden first is the winner. This is called a sack race. It is very difficult to do, because it's very easy to fall over with your legs inside a sack. You can't go very fast, either, but it is fun. Who do you think will reach the other side first and win the race? Wally is the quickest, so he has won. Gareth and Wally decide to have another sack race, so that Gareth can have another chance to win.

20 July

Looking out together

There was a house with windows.
Two monkeys lived inside.
And all day long those monkeys
out of the windows spied.

They were extremely happy,
as they looked through the glass,
at birds, bees, houses, trees,
and flowers in the grass.

When I asked them why it was
they looked out more and more,
they asked a simple question:
"What else are windows for?"

21 July

A monkey nurse

Sacha Monkey wants to be a monkey nurse
in a monkey hospital when she grows up.
A monkey nurse is someone who looks after
sick monkeys until they are better. A monkey
nurse is always very kind to sick monkeys.
She brings them food and drinks. And puts
sticking plasters on. And if anybody needs an
injection, a monkey nurse does that, too.
Sacha wants to wear white clothes. Monkey
nurses always wear white. Sacha imagines how
she will look in her monkey nurse's uniform.
I'm sure she'll look lovely!

138

22 July

Sand pies

Milly and Tanya Monkey are playing on the
beach. Do you know what they're doing?
They're making pies. Not real pies, but sand
pies. Milly and Tanya have lots of different
shapes. Fish shapes, boat shapes, and star
shapes. And all sorts of other shapes. Milly and
Tanya put sand in the shapes. Then they
press it down well. This pushes the sand right
into the shapes. Then they turn the shapes
upside down. And look … lovely sand pies.
Milly and Tanya have already made lots of
pies. They're all sitting nicely in a row next to
each other on the sand. But what's that?
A great big wave is coming, creeping gently
up the beach, closer and closer …
Gone are the lovely sand pies. The sea just
came and washed them away. Oh well, they'll
just have to start all over again!

23 July

Clouds

Norman is lying on his back in the grass, looking at the sky. There are lots of clouds floating about. Norman looks at the clouds. One looks a bit like a face. How funny! But the cloud keeps on changing. The wind blows it into different shapes. Look, the cloud now looks like an animal. A monkey. Norman looks at another cloud. It looks like a monkey, too, but a small one. Isn't that nice! It looks like a whole family of monkeys up there in the sky!

24 July

Coloured shoes

I know a jolly monkey,
his name is Monkey Biff,
and one day someone gave him
a very lovely gift.

A pair of shoes they gave him,
such special shoes, they said.
They were two different colours,
one green, and one bright red!

The green was for his left foot,
the red was for his right.
Biff's very special coloured shoes
were quite a splendid sight!

25 July

Lemonade with a straw

Imogen and Meg Monkey have been playing outside all day. They've come inside, because they are extremely thirsty after all that playing. "Would you like a drink?" asks their mother. "Yes, please," answer Imogen and Meg. "Wait a minute," says Mother, "I'll go and get you something nice." She comes back with two large glasses of lemonade. "There you are," she says, "and there's a surprise, too. Look." Mother puts a straw in each glass. "What is that?" asks Imogen. "That is a straw," says Mother. "When you put the straw in your mouth and suck on it, the lemonade comes up the straw and into your mouth." "Really?" asks Meg. "Really and truly," replies Mother. "Try it and see." Imogen and Meg put the straws in their mouths and begin to suck. Yes, it works! The lemonade comes into their mouths all by itself! What a nice idea, lemonade with a straw.

26 July

The big wave

Richard Monkey is out swimming.
He's swimming in the sea. Not far out at
sea, because that would be dangerous.
Richard is swimming close to the beach.
You often find the best waves there.
Sometimes there are really big waves.
They are good for diving into. There's a
big wave coming now. Richard stretches
his arms out in front of him and jumps.
Right under the wave. He comes up for
air. But what has happened? Richard
isn't wearing his swimming trunks
any more. The wave has taken the
swimming trunks away with it!
What a thing to do! Richard has a
good look around. His swimming
trunks have been washed up on the
beach. He goes and gets them quickly
and puts them back on. Nobody saw
him. What a naughty wave. Next time,
Richard had better hold on tight to
his swimming trunks!

27 July

A mosquito

Harry and his cuddly monkey are in bed. They're both asleep. "Bzzz," goes something in the bedroom. It wakes Harry up. "Bzzzz," it goes again. "Bzzzzz." Then it goes quiet. Harry can't hear anything, but he does feel something tickling his arm. He looks down at his arm, but he can't see anything. Then the tickling stops. Harry looks again. What's that on Monkey's nose? A horrid mosquito. Harry flaps his hands and chases the mosquito away. I know, thinks Harry, Monkey and I will slide down right under the covers. Then the horrid mosquito won't be able to get us. But the mosquito flies out of the bedroom. Perhaps he knew what Harry was thinking. Anyway, Harry and his monkey can now go back to sleep in peace.

28 July

The monkey in the cupboard

A monkey in a cupboard lived,
he had a piece of paper,
eraser, pencil (nice and sharp),
oh what a silly caper!

He drew a tree with lots of leaves,
and then, just as I feared,
he used the eraser, rub, rub, rub.
The picture disappeared!

Where did that picture go to?
I really cannot think.
Perhaps next time it will be wise
to draw that tree with ink.

29 July

Hanging out the washing

Fiona is helping Mother. She is helping to hang out the washing. They are hanging the washing on the washing-line. The sun is shining and the clothes will dry quickly. Mother is hanging up the big things and Fiona is doing the small things. The washing-line is very high. Fiona can't reach very well, so she stands on a step-ladder. Fiona hangs the washing on the line with pegs. When the telephone rings, Mother has to go inside to answer it. When she comes back, she says: "I'd better check to see you've done everything properly, Fiona." Then Mother laughs. Silly Fiona has hung her cuddly monkey on the line among the washing!

30 July

Swimming with a safety ring

It is very warm outside. Most of the monkeys who live in the wood are swimming in the lake. Jacob Monkey would like to swim, but he's not very good at swimming yet. But Jacob has found a solution to his problem. He puts a safety ring around his middle, which will keep him afloat. Jacob has a rather splendid safety ring. It looks like a giraffe. Jacob has to blow up the safety ring first, before he puts it on. Once it is on, he can keep hold of the giraffe's neck. Swimming is such fun, thinks Jacob.

31 July

Everything has a shadow

Martin is walking along next to his mother on the pavement. They have been shopping, and are now on their way home. "What is that?" asks Martin, pointing to the ground.
"What do you mean?" asks Mother.
"I mean that black mark on the ground. It moves, but I can't get hold of it," explains Martin.
"That is a shadow," says Mother. "The sun does that. It shines on everything and makes shadows. Look at the ground under the tree. There's another black mark there, just like the one by you. That is the shadow of the tree."
Martin looks at the shadow. "But that mark isn't moving at all," he says, "and my mark is."
"But the tree isn't moving, is it?" says Mother.
When they get home, Martin fetches his cuddly monkey. He wonders if Monkey has a shadow, too. Yes, Mother is right. When Martin moves his monkey, the shadow moves, too. When Martin holds him still, the shadow doesn't move. Don't mothers know a lot!

1 August

The bald monkey

Once upon a time there was
a monkey in Mayfair.
And strange to tell, upon his head
was not a single hair.

His great long tail, his arms, his legs
were all as they should be,
all covered in nice thick, brown fur,
except his head, you see.

Perhaps you will be thinking:
"that's really not so frightful."
But do you really find a monkey
bald as an egg delightful?

2 August

A treasure chest?

John and Marianne are playing up in the attic. It's really messy up there. There are old things everywhere. It even smells a bit old. "Look at this beautiful chest," says John. They try to open it, but they can't. "It's locked," says John, "but the key's in the lock." John turns the key, the chest opens and … there is a lovely cuddly monkey inside, a very big one. "How nice," says Marianne. "I wonder if this was Grandpa's monkey. I bet we're allowed to play with it." So all three of them play all afternoon up in the attic: John, Marianne, and the cuddly monkey.

3 August

Monkeys in love

Paul and Minnie Monkey are out walking in the wood. Paul and Minnie are holding hands. Do you know why? They like each other very much. Sometimes they give each other a kiss. Paul and Minnie are in love. When you are in love, you like someone very much. Paul and Minnie do everything together. They go to school and then they walk home together. Paul and Minnie always play together, too. And sometimes they go for a walk in the wood together. Then they hold hands, just like now. Paul and Minnie like being in love. But some of the other monkeys think they're a bit soppy.

4 August

A creaking branch

It is very warm in the wood. Nearly all the monkeys are swimming in the lake. Jim and Bert Monkey have thought of something fun to do. There is a tree next to the lake. Jim and Bert climb the tree, then jump from a branch into the water. The branch is just like a diving board. Jim goes first. He climbs on the branch and ... splash! Jim does a great big jump into the water. Then Bert climbs the tree. But when he steps onto the branch, it begins to creak. Oh no, the branch breaks off with a crack and falls, with Bert still on it, into the water. Bert gets a bit of a fright. He's lucky he didn't hurt himself. Wasn't Bert foolish? You'd never do a thing like that, would you?

5 August

The lollipop tree

There once were three monkeys,
who lived all by themselves.
One day some magic happened.
Had it been done by elves?
In front of the house where they
lived a great tall tree appeared,
covered in lovely lollipops:
"They must be for us!" they
cheered. They ran out and
shook the branches, and hundreds
of lollipops fell. Then, quick as a
wink they ran inside and ate till they
felt unwell. If you want a tree full
of lollipops at your house, wish very
hard. Sometimes they will grow in
the garden, so you'd better be on
your guard!

6 August

Playing tag

Ricky and Tim are playing outside with a cuddly monkey. "I know," says Ricky,
"let's play tag. You're it, Tim." And he runs away as fast as he can.
But Tim doesn't bother to run after him, he tags Monkey instead. "Monkey is it,"
he says, "so tag me if you can!" And he sits down comfortably in the grass.
They're not really playing tag any more, because Monkey can't possibly
run after Tim, now can he? Isn't that clever of Tim?

149

7 August

Heidi's dog

Heidi has a dog called Ben. Heidi looks after Ben very well. She gives him good food and takes him out for lots of walks. Dogs like being taken out for lots of walks. Then they can run and jump about. Heidi plays with Ben, too. She throws a stick for Ben and he fetches it. Heidi and Ben both like that game. Heidi throws the stick as far away as she can, but it falls in the water! Ben rushes after it and comes back dripping wet. Heidi laughs. "Oh, Ben," she says, "you look just like a monkey with all that wet fur!"

8 August

Roller skates

Gus has been given a pair of roller skates. They're a bit like ice skates with little wheels underneath. You can skate on the pavement in them. Gus has only just got them, but he's quite good at skating already. Gus puts one foot very carefully in front of the other. And he's off! Oh dear, there's a tree in his path and Gus doesn't know how to brake. What a hard crash that was!
Gus stops roller skating for a little while. He's a bit tired. He goes home and has a rest on the sofa with his cuddly monkey. He reads aloud to his monkey from his favourite book. Then he's ready to go roller skating again.

9 August

One big and one small foot

Once there was a monkey,
who had odd sized feet.
One foot was extremely big,
the other small and neat.

"I've one big and one small foot,
whatever shall I do?
I always have to go barefoot.
I'm sad, no shoes, boo hoo!"

One day he met a cobbler,
who said he didn't mind.
He'd make odd shoes exactly right.
Now wasn't that cobbler kind?

10 August

Counting fingers

"Can you count, yet?" Ellie asks Josephine.
"A bit," replies Josephine.
"I can count to five," says Ellie.
"Five?" says Josephine in amazement, "how?"
"Well," says Ellie, "I just look at the fingers on my hand. I begin with my thumb. That's one. Then I just carry on counting." Ellie points to the next finger on her hand. "That is number two." Then she continues. "Three, four, and my little finger is five!"
"I can count to five, too," says Josephine, "but I don't do it your way. Look, I've got one, two, three dolls, and four, five cuddly monkeys."

11 August

Blowing up balloons

Tom and Richard are blowing up balloons. It's making their faces red. But the balloons are beautiful. Each balloon has a picture of a monkey, an elephant, or a camel on it. The boys are allowed to hang the balloons up in the sitting room. Tomorrow is Mother's birthday and the house must look nice. There will be a party tomorrow, with a delicious cake and a room full of balloons. Tom and Richard had better get blowing!

12 August

A dream

Josh is in bed asleep. And, while he is sleeping, his cuddly monkey jumps off his bed and says to Josh: "So long, Josh, I'm off to live with another little boy. I think I've been with you long enough."
"No," shouts Josh, "don't. Please don't go away!"
Then Josh opens his eyes. It is still dark, but he can see his cuddly monkey lying there on the bed beside him. Oh what a relief! It was all a dream. His cuddly monkey isn't going away at all, he's going to stay with Josh for ever and ever.

13 August

A monkey with glasses

There once was a monkey
whose eyesight was bad.
He hardly saw a single thing,
which made him very sad.

He went to see the doctor,
who cried: "Look, lads and lasses,
it's obvious what the answer is,
you need a pair of glasses!"

So the monkey got some glasses,
not just one pair, but two.
"Thank you, doctor," said the monkey,
"I can see now, thanks to you."

14 August

A flying monkey

Angela is bored. All her friends have gone away and it's too hot to do anything. Mother is busy, too. Angela picks up Arnold Monkey and goes out into the garden. She throws Arnold up into the air. Flop, goes Arnold, as he hits the grass. Angela laughs. Arnold can fly! So she throws him up into the air again. But oh dear! Arnold doesn't land on the grass this time. Poor old Arnold gets stuck on the branch of a tree. Now Angela will have to climb up the tree to get him out. Oh well, at least she's not bored any more!

15 August

Torn swimming trunks

Flip Monkey is swimming in the river. It is very warm today. There are lots of monkeys down by the river. Some monkeys are swimming, others are sunning themselves on the riverbank. Flip is in the water. He swims to the side. He's hungry after all that swimming. He's going to get something to eat. He climbs out of the water and walks over to his towel. But what's that? All the other monkeys are laughing. Flip doesn't see anything to laugh at. He looks around. All the other monkeys are looking at him and laughing even louder. Flip takes a good look at himself and then at his swimming trunks.

Now he understands why everyone is laughing. There is a great big hole in his swimming trunks. Right on his bottom. Then Flip laughs about it himself. It does look funny, a hole in his trunks right in the middle of his backside!

16 August

Chris Monkey on the train

Have you ever been on a train? Chris Monkey has. Chris went on a big yellow and green train. He went to visit Grandma. Mother Monkey went, too. First they had to buy their tickets at the station. The train was waiting there at the station, so they got on straight away. Chris was allowed to sit by the window so he could see out. Then the train set off, going faster and faster. Chris saw all sorts of things through the window: grass and cows, houses and trees. They all whizzed past very quickly. Then along came a man in a uniform who wanted to see Chris's ticket. Grandma Monkey was waiting at the station when they arrived. Chris enjoyed his train journey. He's looking forward to the return journey already.

17 August

The fussy monkey

There once was a monkey, a most fussy monkey,
who wouldn't eat carrots or beans.
He wouldn't eat parsnips,
he wouldn't eat turnips,
and completely refused to eat greens.
He didn't like anything (not even ice-cream),
or fabulous strawberry whips.
When asked what he'd eat,
he'd say: "Listen here, Pete,
just give me a burger and chips!"

Buried

John and Nigel are on the beach. Father and Mother are there, too. Mother is reading and Father is asleep. "I know what we'll do," says John, "let's bury my monkey in the sand." So they do. Two big spadefuls of sand, and the monkey has disappeared. Then John pretends to cry. Father wakes up and Mother looks up from her book. "I've lost my monkey," wails John. "I can't find him anywhere." Father and Mother begin to look, under the towel, in the bag, everywhere. Then John bursts out laughing. "Here he is!" he shouts, "I've magicked him back!"
Mother laughs, too. "You little rascal," she says, "you'd better let me read in peace from now on, or who knows what might really happen to your monkey!"

19 August

Rowing

Albert's father has a boat. It doesn't have a sail, it is a rowing boat. There is a seat in the boat and two oars. You put the oars in the water. Then you move them backwards and forwards to make the boat move. This is called rowing. When it is nice weather, Albert and his father go out rowing in their rowing boat. Albert's monkey is sometimes allowed to go, too. Albert loves going with his father. And, if he is very good, he helps with the rowing. He finds it difficult, but he can manage if Father rows, too. The monkey justs sits and enjoys himself. He's glad he needn't do any of the hard work.

20 August

The goldfish

Martha Monkey has a pet. She has a fish, a goldfish. The fish isn't really made of gold, but it is a lovely orange colour and when it catches the sun, it shines as beautifully as if it were made of gold. It swims around in a glass bowl, so you can see it easily. Martha sits and watches her goldfish a lot. The goldfish opens and closes his mouth. Martha copies. She opens her mouth wide, then closes it. But she doesn't make a noise, because neither does the fish. It looks as if they're talking to each other, but they're not really. Isn't that funny?

21 August

The monkey in the bath

There once was a monkey,
who sat in the tub.
He picked up the soap,
and he started to rub.

He washed his hands,
and under his nails.
Not forgetting, of course,
to wash his tail.

He washed his hair,
then remembered his feet.
Splish splosh, splish splosh,
isn't that monkey clean and neat?

22 August

Marbles

Tom and Simon are playing marbles. They have made a little hollow in the sand.
They must roll their marbles so that they go into this hollow. After a quarter of an
hour, Tom has lost all his marbles to Simon. He has nothing left. Or has he?
Yes, he's still got his cuddly monkey.
"If I lose this time, you may have my monkey," he says to Simon. Simon agrees.
He'd be quite happy to win Tom's monkey! But he doesn't, because Tom wins back
all his marbles. He's very happy, because he didn't really want to part with his
monkey in the first place.

23 August

Washing the car

Keith and his father are washing the
car together. The car is very dirty,
covered in sand and mud. Keith
and Father wash all the mud off.
They both have a sponge. And
there is a big bucket of soapy
water. Keith dips the sponge in
the soapy water, then wipes the
car. Keith wipes the sponge back
and forth, back and forth, and in
no time the car is covered with foam
instead of sand and mud. Father
fetches the garden hose and sprays
the foam off. Only then does Keith
notice that his cuddly monkey is
all wet. He had put him down
next to the car.
Father laughs. "That was very clever
of us," he says, "we've killed two
birds with one stone. We've washed
the car and your monkey in one go.
Now they can both dry in the sun!"

24 August

In the sand pit

Melvin and Nicola are playing in the sand pit. They are doing something very difficult: they are making a sand monkey. Nicola's monkey is sitting next to them, because he is the model. Melvin keeps fetching buckets of water from the kitchen. It makes the sand stick together better. At last the monkey is finished. The sand monkey is nearly as good as the real monkey. Mother is amazed when she comes to look.
"You've done it beautifully," she says. "I think you must be sand sculptors!"

25 August

Skipping

"Look what I've been given," says Ellen to her friend Wendy. "A skipping rope. Do you want to skip with me?" Both Ellen and Wendy are very good at skipping. "This is too easy," says Ellen after a bit, "I wonder how we can make it a bit more difficult?" She goes inside and comes back with a monkey and a doll. "Right, now Monkey and Dolly have to skip, too," she says. Wendy goes first and is out straight away, because the rope catches on Dolly's leg. I don't think Dolly is really in the mood for skipping, do you?

26 August

A swimming pool in the garden

"Mother, I'm so hot!" says Boris. "Please may I go swimming?" But Boris is too small to go to the swimming pool on his own. Mother thinks about it. Then she says: "I've thought of something. Wait a minute." She goes and gets a big tub and puts it on the grass. Then she fills it with water, right up to the top. "Look," says Mother, "now we've got a swimming pool in our garden." Boris has his clothes off in no time and gets into the tub with his cuddly monkey. Now he's not hot any more. Wasn't Mother clever to think of this? Boris and his monkey stay in their own little swimming pool all afternoon.

27 August

A fly in the custard?

Otto and David Monkey are sitting at the kitchen table. They have just eaten their supper. Mother gives them both a bowl of custard. "Mmmm, yummy!" says Otto, "custard." Just as he is about to take a mouthful, David shouts, "Look out! There's a fly in your custard."

"Where?" asks Otto, and bends his head down to his bowl to look for the fly. He can't see any fly. "There isn't a …" But Otto doesn't get a chance to finish his sentence because David pushes his head right down into the custard. Otto's face is covered in custard. "Yuck," he says, "very funny, David, very funny indeed. So funny, in fact, that you haven't even noticed the fly in your own custard."

"There's no fly in my custard!" says David. "Oh yes, there is!" says Otto, "have a good look." So David bends his head down to look at his bowl, and yes, you've guessed already, Otto pushes David's nose into his custard, too. David's nose is all yellow. Mother comes into the room. "What are you two doing?" she asks.

"Oh, nothing," says Otto, "we thought we saw flies in our custard, but there weren't any!" Mother doesn't understand. But Otto and David do. They fall about laughing.

28 August

The monkey on the tightrope

Listen here, listen here,
to what I have to tell,
about a monkey, brave and good,
who walked a tightrope in a wood,
and did it very well.
Now listen here, now listen here,
to what I have to tell.
That monkey walked high in the sky,
with steady foot and steady eye,
and never, ever fell!

29 August

On a big boat

Pete Monkey is on a boat with lots of other monkeys. The boat isn't going very fast, but that doesn't matter. Pete is looking at the water and the waves the boat makes. He looks up at the birds in the sky, too. The captain is the boss on board ship and is wearing a beautiful cap. The cap shows that he is the captain. Pete thinks he might like to be a ship's captain when he is grown up. He thinks it would be fun. Then he could wear a captain's cap, too.

30 August

Flowers for Grandma Monkey

Look, there is Annie Monkey.
What's that there in her hand?
Who are those lovely flowers for?
It must be someone grand.

Where are you going, Annie?
Who are the flowers for?
"I'm going to see my Grandma,
I hear her back is sore.

"I'll put them in a vase,
perhaps I'll write a letter.
Maybe, when she gets it,
my Grandma will be better."

31 August

A monkey from the wood

Jacob Monkey lives in a very big wood.
Lots of other monkeys live there, too, as do
lots of Jacob's friends. They all play together
every day. They swoosh down the branches
of the trees and steal bananas. Jacob thinks
his wood is the nicest wood in all the world.
He'll never move, he's sure of that. No, he'll
stay with his friends and play games every
day. Jacob is so tired each evening that he
just falls asleep on a branch of a tree. He
wakes up at sunrise, then begins to play
again. Jacob plays all day and every day. I
wish I were a monkey. Then I could climb
trees and play all day. But I can't, because
whereas monkey children may play all day
if they wish to, human children sometimes
have to go to school.

163

1 September

Going to school

Sebastian is going to school today for the first time. His mother is taking him there. Sebastian is a bit scared. He would really prefer to stay at home and play outside. There are lots of other children at school and a teacher, too. When he goes into the classroom, Sebastian holds Yoyo his cuddly monkey very tightly. He is glad that his mother let him take Yoyo with him. Now he doesn't have to go into school all by himself. Perhaps he'll be brave enough to go in on his own tomorrow. Then Yoyo can stay at home with Mother.

2 September

The green monkey

A monkey was born a long way away,
his father's name was Abdullah.
What made him different in every way
was his very unusual colour.

Now most monkeys are brown
from their toes to their crown,
but he was a sight to be seen.
From right at the top
and then all the way down,
this monkey was totally green!

An ant-hill

Hunky and Thomas Monkey are out walking in the wood. They've already walked a long way and Hunky is a bit tired. "I must stop for a rest," he says, "I'm so tired!" He goes to sit down on a hump. "Don't!" shouts Thomas, "don't sit there! That's no ordinary hump of earth. That's an ant-hill."
"An ant-hill?" says Hunky with surprise. "What's that?"
"An ant-hill is a heap of earth where thousands of ants live. It is an ant house. They don't like it if someone sits on their house, because it will be broken. Then the ants will try to make you go away by running all over your arms and legs."
"Yuck," says Hunky, "I bet that would itch."
"If you look closely," says Thomas, "you can see the ants running about. They have made lots of tunnels in the ant-hill." Hunky and Thomas study the ant-hill together. They see some ants running back and forth.
"I'm glad I didn't sit on it," says Hunky, "otherwise the ants would have been really cross." "Yes," says Thomas, "I think so, too."

4 September

Is it raining?

Clara is sitting outside in the sun with her cuddly monkey. Their eyes are closed. Suddenly Clara feels some drops of water on her face. She looks up at the sky. It can't be raining because the sky is blue and there aren't any clouds. She sits down again. Again she feels drops of water on her face. She looks down at her monkey. He has drops of water on his face, too.
Then she sees Melvin. Melvin is hiding behind her chair with a glass of water in his hand. When Clara isn't looking, Melvin shakes some drops of water on her. Clara chases Melvin away. Horrible boy, she thinks. Then she sits down again in her chair to enjoy the sunshine.

5 September

Stilts

Keith Monkey is walking on stilts. A stilt is a long stick with a block of wood attached to it near the bottom. If you have two of them, you can walk around by putting your feet on the blocks and holding onto the sticks. It is quite difficult, because you have to keep your balance and not fall over.
Keith has been practising with his stilts. At first he kept falling off, but he's much better at it now. He puts one stilt in front of the other. He does still wobble a bit sometimes, but he doesn't quite fall over. Well done, Keith!

6 September

Two monkeys

One monkey is extremely big,
the other very small.
One is very hairy,
and the other almost bald.
The first is black as black can be,
the second is quite brown.
The black one sits and scratches,
the brown one jumps around.
One speaks very politely,
the other's very rude,
but both agree that ripe bananas
are their favourite food!

7 September

A rocking chair

Tim is staying at Grandpa's. Grandpa is in the kitchen. He is making supper. Tim is a bit tired, so he sits down for a minute. But his chair begins to wobble! Tim drops his cuddly monkey in fright. "Grandpa, help!" he shouts. "What is the matter?" asks Grandpa. "The chair won't stay still. It wobbles. And my monkey has fallen onto the floor," says Tim. Grandpa chuckles to himself. "Of course the chair wobbles," he says. "It's a rocking chair. You can rock gently back and forth in it." Tim climbs back into the chair very carefully. Yes, Grandpa was right, it does rock. A few minutes later, Grandpa looks up from his cooking to see Tim and his monkey fast asleep in the rocking chair. They had rocked themselves to sleep. Night night, Tim!

A hedgehog in the garden

"Oh look, there's a ball in the garden," says Stephen to Anthony. Stephen goes to pick up the ball. "Ouch, this ball is prickly," he says. And the ball begins to move all by itself. A small nose appears out of the ball. And four little legs. Then it begins to walk. "That's not a ball," says Anthony, "that's a hedgehog!" The hedgehog had rolled itself up into a ball and gone to sleep. But hedgehogs, while they may look like balls, have prickles. When Stephen tried to pick up the ball, he pricked himself on the prickles. Anthony thinks it's quite funny and laughs. He goes inside to fetch his cuddly monkey. He sits him on the hedgehog's back. It is a very strange sight. The poor hedgehog is a bit frightened. It scurries into the bushes to hide. Stephen runs after it to get his monkey, otherwise he might be lost!

9 September

The calf

Hugo lives on a farm. There are lots of animals on the farm. There are chickens, a cockerel, sheep, and cows. Hugo's father has a lot of cows. One day, Bella the cow gives birth to a calf. A calf is a sweet baby cow. Hugo thinks it is so sweet that he would like to take it to bed with him. But he's not allowed to. Father says the calf is far too big to fit in Hugo's bed. No, Hugo must be content with Charlie, his cuddly monkey. He fits easily in Hugo's bed. And the new calf really needs to stay with its mother in the meadow. Then everyone will get some sleep. Hugo may go and look at the calf every day. He takes Charlie along with him for company.

10 September

A golden crown

There once was a monkey
who said: "I'd like to be
a little bit different
from the likes of you and me."

So he went to a shop
(on the other side of town),
and there saw what he wanted:
a lovely golden crown!

He put the crown upon his head,
and said: "Now look at that.
Isn't that a great deal better
than an ordinary hat?"

11 September

Banana bobbing

Fenella and Jasper Monkey were rather bored. Mother has thought of a good game for them to play. She has hung a rope between two trees, and tied pieces of banana to the rope. Fenella and Jasper must try to get the pieces of banana. But not with their hands. No, they must keep their hands behind their backs. They must try to get the pieces of banana with their mouths. The game is called banana bobbing. It's fun to play and the bananas taste lovely. If you can get them.
Fenella and Jasper stand next to the rope with their hands behind their backs.
Fenella stands on tiptoes. She bites into a piece of banana. Yes, she's got it!
Jasper's got one, too. What a funny way to eat a banana!

12 September

Time for a photograph

Maggie has a camera. It's not a real camera. It's a trick camera that you can fill with water. When you press the button to take a picture of someone, the camera squirts water at them. But nobody knows that at first. "Mother," says Maggie, "shall I take a photograph of you and my monkey?" Mother picks up Maggie's monkey and smiles for the camera. Maggie holds the camera up to her face. She presses the button and … a squirt of water comes out. Mother and the monkey are dripping wet. Maggie thinks it's terribly funny. Mother hadn't expected that!

13 September

The see-saw

It is beautiful weather and Dominic wants to play outside. He gets his toy monkey Chunky and goes out into the garden. He can't decide what to do. Yes, he's thought of something. He's going to go on the see-saw with Chunky. Dominic sits Chunky on one end, then sits on the other end himself. But nothing happens. Chunky stays up in the air. "That's not fair, Chunky," says Dominic, "now it's my turn to be up in the air." Silly Dominic. He doesn't realize that he is much heavier than Chunky so his end of the see-saw will never go up in the air!

172

14 September

Wally Monkey

I'm a monkey called Wally,
my house is up a tree.
Please can I persuade you
to climb up and visit me?

Sitting here can be lonely,
as dull as dull can be.
That is why I'm asking:
please come and play with me.

First I'll go up the ladder.
Then you follow behind.
We'll both have tea and muffins.
Isn't that so kind!

15 September

A scary animal?

Carolyn is in bed asleep. Her curtains are open and the moon is shining into her bedroom. Suddenly Carolyn wakes up. She looks around her room and jumps with fright. Whatever is that? It looks as if there's a scary animal sitting on her chair. Oh no, what should she do? At first she slides down under the covers, but the animal on the chair doesn't move. She decides to get out of bed and creeps slowly and silently over to her chair. Then she begins to laugh. It isn't a scary animal at all, it's just friendly old Keith, her cuddly monkey. Silly Carolyn had completely forgotten that she had put him there herself before she went to bed.

16 September

The bath is leaking!

Freddy is in the bath. It is a big bath. Freddy has already washed himself, but Mother has said he may stay in the bath and play for a while. Freddy is playing with some little toy monkeys in the bath. He has a toy boat, too. He lets the monkeys sail on the boat in the bath.

But what's that on the bottom of the bath? It looks like a chain. Freddy pulls the chain. What's happening? All the water starts to run out of the bath. Freddy has pulled out the plug. Oh well, he'll just have to continue his game tomorrow.

17 September

Bossy Rudy

Rudy Monkey is often bossy. He tells the other monkeys what to do. Rudy's mother has told him lots of times that he must listen to the others and stop being so bossy. Rudy knows really that he shouldn't be so bossy. He doesn't do it on purpose. It's as if he can't help it. Rudy does try hard to be nice to the other monkeys, but it doesn't always work. Perhaps he'll learn one day. What do you think?

18 September

A gold tooth

There once lived a monkey
in Redruth, I'm told,
and guess what? That monkey
had one tooth of gold.

To see that gold tooth clearly,
all you had to do
was start to laugh very loudly,
and he would then laugh, too.

He was extremely famous,
and really very grand,
tourists came to see him,
unique in monkeyland!

19 September

A conjuror

Father is taking Suzie and Davey to the circus. What fun! There are elephants, and
bears, and lions, and an acrobat. But the conjuror is the best. All he has is a hat, and
what do you think he conjures out of it? A monkey, a real, live monkey! The monkey
squeaks and goes and sits on the conjuror's head. Then the conjuror conjures the
monkey back into his hat. Suzie and Davey have no idea how he did it.
Wherever has the monkey gone?

20 September

Puppet show

Sebastian Monkey is at school. Something special is happening at school today. The teacher is doing a puppet show. The puppet theatre is already in the classroom. The curtains are still closed. But when it's time for the show, the curtains will open to show all the puppets. All the monkeys in the class are sitting on benches in front of the puppet theatre. And look, the curtains are opening. A puppet pops out. "Hello, everybody," says the puppet. "Hello," shout back all the monkeys. The puppet begins to tell a story and introduces the other puppets. Sebastian is really enjoying the puppet show and so are the other monkeys. At last the show is over. The curtains close again. Sebastian thinks it's a shame the show has finished. But perhaps the teacher will do it again one day. Wouldn't that be nice?

21 September

Autumn begins

It is a special day in the monkey wood, because autumn begins today. The sun doesn't shine quite so much in the autumn, and the weather gets colder. Everything changes in the wood. Autumn changes the colours of the leaves from green to yellow, orange, red, and brown. Then they fall from the trees to the ground. There are leaves everywhere in the wood. But not just leaves. There are acorns, horse chestnuts, sweet chestnuts, and beech nuts, too. Some of the woodland monkeys go collecting acorns or mushrooms. Mushrooms grow in the autumn. Sometimes it rains or is very windy. If it is bad weather, all the monkeys huddle together to keep warm. And when the sun comes out again, they carry on collecting their acorns and mushrooms.

22 September

Prince Roderick

Do you know Roderick Monkey?
He's upper class you know,
He speaks extremely nicely,
the papers tell us so.

He's lots and lots of money,
lives in a castle large.
They say it has a hundred rooms,
to visit there's a charge!

He also has a lot of clothes,
a crown sits on his head.
I do believe the crown stays on
when he goes up to bed.

He has a splendid pony,
rides daily in the park,
but never in the evening
for he doesn't like the dark!

At the toy shop

Simone and Grandma are in the toy shop. Grandma has said that Simone may choose a toy for herself. Simone doesn't know what to choose. There are so many lovely things in the shop. Should she have that big doll with the blue eyes? Or the train set, or the boat, or that doll's house?

Suddenly Simone spots a toy monkey sitting on a shelf. "That's what I would like, please, Grandma, that monkey," she says.

"Are you quite sure?" asks Grandma. "Wouldn't you prefer that lovely doll's house?" No, Simone has decided on the monkey. When they are outside the shop, she says to Grandma: "Do you know why I chose him? Because he was the nicest toy in the whole shop."

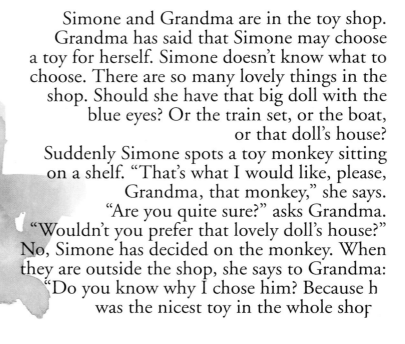

24 September

Sticking plaster on your mouth!

Lisa is in the kitchen and just won't stop talking. She talks and talks. Lisa is never short of something to talk about. Sometimes that can be nice, but sometimes it drives you up the wall. Lisa's mother has been listening to Lisa's chatter all day. She's had enough. "I know what I'm going to do with you," says Mother, "I'm going to put a sticking plaster on your mouth if you don't stop talking!" That doesn't sound very nice to Lisa. Just to see how it looks, she puts a sticking plaster on her monkey's mouth. No, that can't be very nice, because it makes her monkey look sad. Lisa takes off the sticking plaster straight away. All right then, she thinks, perhaps I had better stop talking for a bit.

25 September

Soup with string?

"Supper's ready!" calls Mother Monkey. Father and Tom Monkey come into the
kitchen and they all sit down at the table. Mother puts bowls of soup on the table.
They're all hungry. Tom puts his spoon into the soup. He starts to take a mouthful.
But then he looks at his spoon. "What are those funny stringy things?" he asks.
"That is vermicelli," replies Mother. "Vermiwhat?" asks Tom.
"Vermicelli," repeats Mother patiently. "It's very nice. Try it." Tom takes a mouthful.
Yummy! "May we have soup with string again tomorrow?" asks Tom.

26 September

The biscuit tin

There once was a monkey,
who lived in Deal,
and biscuits from a biscuit tin
he always used to steal.

He did it very carefully,
so that nobody saw,
because he knew so very well
it was against the law.

But one day Mother caught him,
Father was there as well.
"That's not the right way to behave,"
they said, "now listen well."

"Never, never, never, never,
make the big mistake
of taking what you're welcome to,
just ask before you take!"

27 September

To the zoo

Maria and Grandpa are going to the zoo. "What shall we look at first?" asks Grandpa after he has paid to go in. "The monkeys," says Maria. The monkeys live in a monkey house. It's raining today, so they're all inside. "Oh look, Grandpa!" says Maria, "can you see that little monkey there by its mother? Isn't it sweet?" Maria wants to stay by the monkeys all afternoon. Then she'll go and look at the other animals another day.

28 September

Squeak!

A monkey sat upon a stick,
behind the kitchen door.
A funny place to sit, you'd say,
well wait, I'll tell you more.

That monkey wears a shirt which has
a hole somewhere behind,
and through that hole he puts his tail.
He doesn't seem to mind.

So now his long, long tail can hang
right down and touch the floor.
But still I don't know why he sits
behind the kitchen door.

29 September

The monkey doctor

Charles wants to be a monkey doctor when he is bigger. Do you know why? Charles would like to make sick monkeys better. And you can do that if you're a monkey doctor. Charles would like to wear a doctor's white coat. But if you want to be a monkey doctor, you have to study for a very long time first. You have to learn lots and lots of things. Including how to make sick monkeys better. Charles doesn't mind going to school one bit. Because then, perhaps, he might be able to make all the monkeys in the zoo better when he's older.

30 September

A monkey in the rain

Spitter spatter, spitter spatter,
I'm walking in the rain.
I haven't got my boots on,
silly, silly me!

Spitter spatter, spitter spatter,
I'm walking in the rain.
I haven't got a raincoat on,
silly, silly me!

Spitter spatter, spitter spatter,
I'm walking in the rain.
It's pouring down, I'm soaking wet,
silly, silly me!

1 October

The monkey from Paradise

In a place called Paradise
lives a monkey they call Snappy.
He's living there with seven mice.
They seem to be extremely happy.

They always play together.
"Having lots of fun," they said.
And when it's night they go to sleep
in one enormous bed.

So should you see a monkey
in bed with seven mice,
you'll recognize our Snappy,
the ape from Paradise.

2 October

In the garden

Janey, her mother, and Coco the toy monkey are in the garden. Janey is allowed to help Mother prune. Mother has given her a small pair of shears and shows her which branches and twigs to cut off. Mother has a large pair of shears and even Coco has his own tiny shears. Mother told Janey that some bushes grow better if they are cut back, or pruned, in the autumn. When spring comes, Janey may help again in the garden, because then it will be time to prune some other bushes. Janey likes being out in the garden. So does Coco.

The roof is leaking!

Vincent is eating a sandwich in the kitchen. He can't play outside because it is raining heavily. Then he hears a noise. Drip, drip, goes the noise. It sounds as if it's raining inside. Vincent looks around. He notices a small pool of water on the floor. Right in the middle of the pool of water is his toy monkey. Monkey is dripping wet. Then Vincent looks up at the ceiling. He sees a droplet of water hanging there. Vincent rushes off to get his father. Father looks at the droplet of water on the ceiling, too. "Oh dear," he says, "I think the roof is leaking." Father goes to inspect the roof. Luckily there is only a small hole, and he is able to fix it. "That's that," he says. "No more water will get through there today." Wasn't it lucky that Vincent noticed the pool of water? Otherwise the whole kitchen might have been flooded.

4 October

A party in the wood

There is a big party today in the wood. The animals have decorated everywhere. Red, yellow, blue, and purple streamers are hanging in the trees. All the monkeys are wearing party hats and bows on their tails. The elephants have tied bows around their trunks. The giraffes have gone one better and each tied several different coloured bows around their long necks. Today is animal day. It's a sort of birthday for all the animals. So they decided to celebrate, making music and singing songs. There are lots of delicious things to eat, too. The party lasts the whole day, and even the smallest monkey is allowed to stay up late.

5 October

Trumpet

Whatever is that noisy noise?
Taran-taran-tara!
It sounds just like a trumpet,
taran-taran-tara!

It is a trumpet playing.
Taran-taran-tara!
(No, not a donkey braying.)
Taran-taran-tara!

6 October

The mousetrap

Billie's mother has put a mousetrap in the kitchen. If you put a piece of cheese in a mousetrap, the mice will try and get it. Then, when the mouse bites into the cheese, the trap is sprung and the mouse is caught. Billie doesn't want Mother to catch the mice in the kitchen. She likes having them there. So she secretly takes the cheese out of the mousetrap very carefully, then puts it into the mousehole. The mice are very pleased and eat the cheese. That's better, thinks Billie, and sits down to play next to the mousehole with her doll and her cuddly monkey.

7 October

A shooting star

Oliver is in bed, but he can't sleep. He tosses and turns. His monkey keeps getting in the way and annoying him. Oliver gets up and goes over to the window. It is very dark outside. Then, suddenly, Oliver sees a shooting star. The star makes a trail through the night sky for a moment and is gone. Oliver remembers that if you see a shooting star you may make a wish. So he wishes that he could get to sleep. Then he goes back to bed. The minute his head touches the pillow, Oliver falls asleep. Next time you see a shooting star, don't forget to make a wish. Well, Oliver's wish came true, didn't it?

8 October

Picking apples

Lisa Monkey is at Grandma and Grandpa's. Grandma and Grandpa have a very big garden. There are apple trees with lots of apples on them. The apples are nearly ripe and ready to be picked and eaten. A few days later the apples are ripe enough, and Grandpa Monkey decides it's time to pick them. Lisa is allowed to help. Grandpa puts a ladder up against an apple tree so that he can reach the apples easily. Lisa puts the apples in a basket. Every now and again she helps herself to one of the delicious apples. Nobody minds, because there are such a lot.

9 October

Ingrid Monkey

Who is this approaching?
Which monkey's coming near?
Oh, Ingrid Monkey, is it you?
Where have you been, my dear?

Now why are you so dirty
with mud from head to toe?
You really should be careful
where you put your feet, you know.

"Well," said Ingrid Monkey,
"I was standing by the brook,
I thought that I could fly across.
I fell in, and now look!"

10 October

Barbed wire

Miriam and her toy monkey are in the field with the horse. There is a barbed wire fence right around the field so that the horse can't escape. When Miriam has finished stroking the horse she decides to go home. Very carefully, she creeps under the barbed wire fence. But not carefully enough, because her monkey gets caught. He has a great big tear in his trousers. Oh dear, thinks Miriam, Mother will be angry. She runs the rest of the way home. Mother isn't too cross, but Miriam has to promise never to go under the barbed wire again.

187

11 October

Dancing together

Fenella and Jasper Monkey are sitting under a big tree in the wood.
"I know what we can do," says Fenella, "we can dance!"
"Dance?" says Jasper, surprised. "That's no fun."
"Oh yes, it is!" says Fenella and begins to hum a tune. A monkey tune.
Then she begins to dance.
"Come on, Jasper," she says. Jasper doesn't really want to, but he gets up.
"I don't know how to dance," he says.
"Just watch me," says Fenella. She moves her legs and jigs from one foot to
the other. She waves her arms about, then does a little spin. "There, you see,
it's not a bit difficult." Jasper has a go. He copies Fenella exactly. And dances!
"Hey," says Jasper, "this is fun!"
"What did I tell you?" says Fenella, and they carry on dancing
together until they are too tired to dance any more.

12 October

My monkey's blowing away!

It is raining, and Frank is walking down the street. He has just bought a lovely, big, cardboard monkey in the toy shop. This monkey can stand up straight with its tail in the air. The idea is to throw rings so that they land on his tail. It is very windy. A gust of wind wrenches the monkey out of Frank's hands. A man walking down the street just manages to catch the monkey before it flies out of reach. Who knows, perhaps the monkey might have been blown on the wind all the way to China!

13 October

Curly head

A monkey sat and cried one day,
and said: "It isn't fair.
I really, really, really, really
wish I'd curly hair."

"No problem," said the hairdresser,
"just sit down in this chair."
And half an hour later,
he had lovely curly hair.

So now there's no more crying,
(not until he gets back home),
for curly hair is nice to see,
but very hard to comb.

14 October

Hopscotch

Betty and Katy are playing hopscotch. They have drawn some squares on the ground, and now they must try to jump from one to the other. On one leg. This is called hopping. Jacko Monkey is playing, too, but he's very bad at hopping. So Betty throws him right the way down to the last square. "Look, Katy," she laughs, "Jacko has hopped all the way to the final square. Isn't he clever?"

15 October

A paper monkey

Tim is sitting at the table with Grandpa. They are making things from paper. Grandpa is folding a piece of paper into the shape of a monkey. Tim is watching very carefully, because it is very difficult to do. But Grandpa is very clever and, before Tim has been able to work out how it was done, the monkey is finished. Tim is allowed to colour in the monkey, then hang it on the wall in his bedroom. While he is colouring, Tim decides that he would also like an elephant, a giraffe, and a big lion! Grandpa's going to be busy, isn't he?

16 October

The photograph album

Davey is sitting on the sofa with Mother. They are looking at a photograph album.
In the album are photographs of Davey when he was a baby.
"Look," says Mother, "that was taken just after you were born."
"Is that me?" asks Davey, surprised.
"Yes," says Mother, "that's you."
"But that can't be me," says Davey, feeling his head, "because I've got lots of hair
and that baby is almost bald!"
"Yes, I know," laughs Mother, "but most babies have very little hair when
they are born. It grows later."
There is a photograph of a very small boy with a big, soft, cuddly monkey.
"Look," says Mother, "that's you, too, with Fluffy Monkey."
Davey has to believe Mother this time, because he recognizes his monkey, Fluffy.
"Look, Mother," he says, "Fluffy was almost as big as me then, and now
I'm much bigger than Fluffy."
Mother laughs. "That's because little boys grow and toy monkeys don't!"

17 October

Sebastian Monkey

There once was a monkey
with very little hair.
Instead of growing everywhere
it just grew here and there.

He put a great big hat on
and thought himself a toff.
So proud was he of his new hat
He never took it off.

"Take a look. I am Sebastian,
the monkey with the hat,
with nice red bow and ribbon.
What do you think of that?"

18 October

A toadstool

There is a lovely big toadstool in Jenny's garden. Jenny is lying down on the grass looking at it. Grandpa told her that a tiny monkey lives in the toadstool, so she is waiting for it to come out. "Monkey," she calls, "won't you come outside and play? I'd like to be your friend." But nothing happens. Later, when Mother comes out into the garden, she says: "Oh Jenny, Grandpa just made that up. There's no little monkey in that toadstool. If you go inside there's a mug of chocolate milk waiting for you." Jenny is a bit disappointed about the monkey, but she's quite happy to have a mug of chocolate milk.

19 October

The colouring competition

Anita is sitting at the kitchen table. She is colouring a drawing with crayons. She didn't do the drawing herself, she is just colouring it in. She's doing it very neatly, staying inside the lines. The drawing is of a monkey. Anita has given him orange trousers and an orange cap. Whoever does the best colouring of the monkey will win the prize. Anita hopes it will be her.

20 October

Grandma Monkey makes apple sauce

Lisa Monkey is visiting Grandma. On her last visit, Lisa helped Grandpa to pick lots of apples in the garden. There were far too many to eat just like that. Grandma has thought of something to do with all the extra apples. She's going to make apple sauce. First she peels the apples, then she chops them up and puts them in a big pan with some sugar and a little water. She puts the pan on the cooker and cooks the apples until they turn into apple sauce. Lisa loves apple sauce. So does Grandpa. Especially if Grandma has made it herself.

193

21 October

On the bicycle

Look there on that bicycle,
Barry Monkey's going past.
He's very good at cycling,
and goes so very fast.

The pedals they go round and round,
as fast as fast can be.
Here he comes, no, there he goes,
as quick as one, two, three!

22 October

The monkey fight

Barry and Jim are in bed, but they can't get to sleep. "Let's have a monkey fight," suggests Barry. "We'll hit each other with our toy monkeys. They're soft so it won't hurt." So they start bashing each other. Then Jim gives Barry a very hard bang with his monkey, and the poor monkey's arm falls off! Oh dear, Jim is upset. Mother has heard the noise and comes to see what's going on. She sees what has happened straight away. "That wasn't a very nice thing to do, was it, Jim?" she says. "I'll sew Monkey's arm back on just this once, but you must promise never to do this again. Monkeys are not for fighting with." Barry and Jim lie down to go to sleep. The monkey fight was no fun any more, anyway.

23 October

The monkey peep-show

Saskia is making a peep-show from a large shoe-box. A peep-show is a box with lots of interesting things inside and a hole in one end to look through. Saskia starts by making some little trees from paper. Next she makes some monkeys. Then she sticks them in the box. When she has made the hole at the front end, she invites everybody to come and have a look at the monkey wood in her peep-show. It costs a penny a look. Do you think that is expensive?

24 October

The monkey house

Melanie has her nose pressed up against the toy shop window. She is looking at the doll's house. Or I should say the monkey house, because there are little monkeys in it rather than dolls. They look very sweet. Mother pulls Melanie away from the window. "Come on, Melanie, hurry up. We still need to go to the baker's." But Melanie doesn't move. Mother looks at the window display more closely. "They're lovely, aren't they?" she says. "Why don't you put those little monkeys on your birthday present list? It's your birthday soon." Melanie thinks it's a very good idea. She doesn't mind going home now, so that she can start writing her birthday present list.

25 October

What is it?

It's Tom the monkey's birthday,
he's got a lovely gift.
It barks, it has a waggly tail,
it's small enough to lift.

It sniffs at every little thing.
It goes out for a walk.
Whatever could Tom's present be?
I wonder, can it talk?

Is it a dog? Perhaps a cat?
I really cannot tell.
Maybe a rabbit or a mouse.
Could I have one as well?

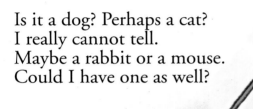

26 October

The runaway

Brian Monkey is out walking in the wood. He has run away from home. He didn't like it at home any more. He looks around. He's not very sure where he is, and it's beginning to rain, too. Brian is cold and wet. It will be nice and warm at home now. Mother will probably be cooking something nice for supper. Brian feels even hungrier when he thinks about food. He wonders where he's going to sleep. He has his own bed at home. Brian thinks about his home. He doesn't really want to run away. So he turns around and goes home as fast as he can. He might even be in time for supper.

27 October

A paper hat

"Guess what I'm going to make?" Grandpa asks Tim. "A paper hat. Look." Grandpa takes a sheet of newspaper and folds it several times. As if by magic, it turns into a hat. Grandpa puts the hat on Tim's monkey's head. It looks good!
"Now a hat for you," says Grandpa. He takes another sheet of newspaper, makes another hat, and puts it on Tim's head. So now both Tim and his monkey have a newspaper hat. What fun!

28 October

The banana skin

Dan is at the zoo. He is eating a banana. When he has finished the banana, he throws the skin on the ground. Seth Monkey is behind Dan. Seth steps on the banana skin and whoosh … slips and falls over. He hurts his bottom on the pavement. Ouch! Seth rubs his bottom. It really does hurt. "Oh dear, I am sorry. That wasn't very nice," says Dan. He picks up the banana skin and throws it in a bin. "There," he says, "nobody else will slip on my banana skin now." They carry on walking round the zoo together. Dan knows better than to throw his banana skins on the ground any more. It can cause accidents.

197

29 October

Filthy weather

Kim, the little monkey,
looks through the window sadly.
She wants to go outside to play,
but it's raining rather badly.

What filthy, filthy weather.
Not raining, no, it's pouring.
The wind is howling through the trees.
Kim thinks it's very boring.

Mother says: "Stop moping.
Come over here to me,
then I will go and rustle up
a lovely cup of tea."

30 October

Raking the leaves

Natalie is in the garden with Father. Father is raking leaves and Natalie is helping him. The leaves are on the ground because it is autumn. They fall off the trees. There are lots and lots of leaves on the ground. Look, there's a whole pile. Natalie rakes the pile of leaves. But what's that? Jacko Monkey appears from under the pile of leaves. Natalie lost him a week ago. Now she knows where he was! Natalie is very happy to have him back again. She runs inside and puts him by the fire to dry. He had got a bit wet and dirty under all those dead leaves.

31 October

Looking for chestnuts

Thomas and Hunky Monkey are in the wood. They are looking for horse chestnuts. When they grow, they are green with prickles. The green, prickly bit is a jacket. This protects the round, brown nut inside.

In the autumn, the horse chestnuts fall from the trees, just like the leaves. Lots of monkeys and children go looking for them in the autumn. Just like Thomas and Hunky.

"I've got one!" shouts out Hunky.

"No, you haven't," says Thomas. "That's an acorn."

"An acorn?" says Hunky surprised, "how do you know?"

"Because an acorn looks different from a horse chestnut, stupid! It's much smaller and a different colour. Look."

Thomas holds up an acorn and a horse chestnut next to each other. Hunky can see the difference clearly. "Yes," he says, "I see what you mean. Now I know what I'm looking for."

So they carry on looking. They carry on and on until they have a bag full of horse chestnuts. Then they go home to play with them.

199

1 November

A sore finger

Otto is doing some carpentry. He is making a bed for his toy monkey.
Monkey always used to sleep with him in his bed, but Otto thinks he's a
bit too big for that sort of thing now. So his monkey needs his own bed.
Otto has found some planks of wood, some nails, and a hammer. He puts
two pieces of wood together, gets a nail, holds it between finger and
thumb, and gives it a hard bang with the hammer. That's one done.
Then Otto goes to hammer in a second nail. But this time he holds his
finger too close to the nail and … bang! Ouch! Otto has hammered
his finger instead of the nail.
Otto runs to tell Mother what has happened. Mother holds Otto's sore
finger under cold, running water from the tap. That helps to ease the
pain a little. Mother sticks a small piece of sticking plaster on Otto's
sore finger. Then she gives the sore finger a kiss. It will be better soon.
Otto has stopped crying. He'll just have to make his monkey's bed
tomorrow. Monkey may sleep in Otto's bed for one more night.

2 November

The made-up monkey

There once was a monkey
who loved to wear lace.
And all the day long
she would make up her face.

Some lipstick just here
and some nail varnish there,
not forgetting, of course,
the pink bow in her hair.

And a necklace of pearls,
a pretty thing to wear.
Isn't she beautiful?
Fit for anywhere!

3 November

Peeling potatoes

Lisa is sitting at the kitchen table with Grandma. Grandma is peeling potatoes. She is very good at it. She manages to get the potato peel off in one long piece. Lisa looks at the potato peel. It's all curly. She picks it up carefully and drapes it round Boris the monkey's neck. "Look, Grandma," she says, "Boris is wearing a necklace." Grandma laughs, but tells Lisa to take the necklace off Boris because the potato peel is dirty.

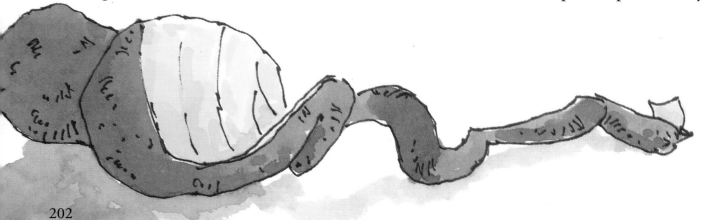

4 November

An unusual garland

Will and Madeleine are sitting at the kitchen table making a garland. A very unusual garland. It is a monkey garland. First, Will folds a piece of paper in half. Then he folds it double several more times. Next he takes scissors and snips bits out of it. When he opens it out, it has turned into a chain of monkeys holding hands. Madeleine is going to colour in the monkeys. She does them all different colours: red, blue, orange, green, and yellow. The monkeys look lovely. When she has finished colouring, they hang their monkey garland up for everyone to admire.

5 November

Lemonade in a monkey?

It was Stevie's birthday yesterday. He got lots of presents. He liked them all, but his favourite present was a monkey beaker. It is a big, white beaker with a picture of a monkey on it. The monkey is wearing a checked jacket and blue trousers. It looks as if he is looking after the drink in the beaker. Mother has filled the new beaker up with lemonade for Stevie. Stevie thinks the monkey is smiling at him as he drinks it. Perhaps the monkey likes lemonade, too.

6 November

Bread with chocolate

There once was a monkey
who, every day,
ate chocolate chip sandwiches.
I couldn't. No way!

He sprinkled the chips
on both sides of the bread.
Some fell out the sides.
"How yummy," he said.

He then put more chocolate
on the crusts as well.
Did it taste good?
Who knows? It's hard to tell.

7 November

Vanity

Diana Monkey is admiring
herself in the mirror. She combs her hair
and ties a bow in it. She puts on her best skirt
and blouse, and smart shoes with bows on.
Then she looks at herself again in the mirror.
She combs her hair a different way, then
studies the effect again in the mirror.
Diana is vain. She spends the whole day
looking at herself in the mirror. All she does is
comb her hair and try on different clothes.
Go on, go and play outside for a while,
Diana, it's much more fun!

8 November

A tent

Paul and Max are playing. They are sitting on the bed with their cuddly toys, a monkey and a bear, and they have made the blankets into a tent. They are pretending they are camping in a big, dark wood. Paul is Mother and Max is Father. Monkey and Bear are the children. "Children," says Mother Paul, "it's time to go to sleep now in the tent. I don't want to hear another sound from you two." So they pretend to go to sleep. It is very quiet in the tent. Because guess what has happened? Paul and Max have really fallen asleep! Night night, campers!

9 November

Bare trees

Tim Monkey is out walking in the wood with Grandpa.

"Golly," says Tim, "aren't the trees bare?"

"Yes," says Grandpa, "that always happens in the autumn. The leaves turn yellow and brown then fall to the ground. Look."

Tim looks at the ground. There are lots of leaves everywhere.

"But will the bare trees get new leaves?" he asks.

"Oh yes," replies Grandpa, "in the spring. When spring comes, new leaves will grow. At first they are just tiny green shoots, but as they grow they turn into proper leaves. Then the tree is green again."

"Oh good," says Tim. "I wouldn't like it if the trees were bare all the time."

10 November

The monkey with hiccups

There once was a poor monkey
who hiccuped all the day.
He held his breath, but no,
the hiccups wouldn't go away.
But then one day an elephant
said: "I know what to do,"
picked up the monkey with his trunk,
and blew a mighty "Boo!"
The elephant said: "Worry no more!
The hiccups have gone, you can be sure."

11 November

A monkey lantern

The children at school are making lanterns today. Sebastian is making one, too. He has made a ball from some special paper and has made two holes in it. These are the eyes. Then he draws a mouth, a nose, and two ears. His lantern is nearly finished. It still needs a stick and a piece of string to hang it up by, and his teacher will put a candle in it. Doesn't it look lovely? The candle light shines out through the eyes. Do you know what Sebastian's lantern looks like? It looks just like a monkey. A monkey lantern.

12 November

Atchoo!

Frank Monkey has a terrible cold. He sneezes all the time. "Atchoo, atchoo," goes Frank. He blows his nose in a big handkerchief. All that blowing gives poor Frank a red nose.
Lots of monkeys get colds in the autumn. "Atchoo," goes Frank again. If you have a very bad cold, you can't smell anything any more. You sometimes lose your sense of taste as well. But colds don't usually last very long, and, once a cold is over, you can smell and taste things again.
"Atchoo!" goes Frank again. Frank really is sneezing a lot. Perhaps he should stay indoors for a while. I'm sure he'll be better soon.

13 November

Drawing on the window

It is very cold outside. Josh is looking outside with his nose pressed up against the window. But that's funny, the window's gone misty. Josh steps back. It's not misty outside, but the window is definitely misty. Do you know why? It was because Josh was breathing warm breath onto the cold glass. This made the window cloud over. Josh decides to draw something on the cloudy window. He draws a monkey. It disappears almost immediately. So Josh breathes on the window again. And draws another monkey. This is fun, he thinks. I can carry on drawing all day like this, and I don't need any paper or pencils!

14 November

Whoops!

There once was a monkey who
by mistake stepped in some pooh.
Once home, he bathed with foam,
and then polished his shoe.

He said to himself: "Silly me!
Fancy treading in pooh, tee hee!
When in the street, I must watch what my feet
are treading in. Don't you agree?"

15 November

Wet through!

Harry and Benny are playing down by the stream.
There is a big tree next to the stream, and from
the tree hangs a long rope. Harry and Benny have
thought up a good game. They tie the rope round
a toy monkey and swing him back and forth over
the stream. This is fun the first couple of times,
but then the rope works itself loose and the poor
monkey falls in the water. Oh dear, how are they
going to get him out? Harry leans forward as far
as he dares and can just reach the monkey with
the tips of his fingers. But the monkey is all
covered in duckweed. Yuck. Now they'll have
to go home and clean him up.

16 November

Not very well

Simon is staying at Grandpa and Grandma's and doesn't feel very well. Not really ill, just not very well. He's actually quite enjoying it, because Grandma comes and reads aloud to him from the big monkey book. Look, here's Grandma now. She's brought the book with her. Simon snuggles down in bed, and Grandma begins to read. She has hardly read more than a few sentences when Simon drifts off to sleep. Oh well, she thinks, no monkey story this time. I wouldn't be surprised if Simon felt much better when he wakes up. What do you think?

17 November

Making monkeys

Meg and Thomas have been to the wood. They have collected lots of acorns and nuts. Now they're sitting at the kitchen table making monkeys out of all the things they have found. They use little, pointy, wooden sticks to make the arms and legs. After an hour or so, the kitchen table is full of monkeys.
"Right," says Thomas, "now we'll make a monkey house at the zoo for all these monkeys." What a good idea!

18 November

A banana fight

Once there were two monkeys,
who lived on the Isle of Wight.
And these two naughty monkeys
held a banana fight.

One threw bananas very well,
he always scored a hit.
The other monkey couldn't seem
to get the hang of it.

And when both tired of fighting,
and it came to time for bed,
they stopped throwing bananas,
and ate them up instead.

19 November

Cream everywhere

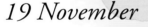

Mother is in the kitchen making a cake.
Lizette is helping. The cake is nearly ready.
It is cooking in the oven.
"Please may I whip the cream?" asks Lizette.
She may. Mother puts the cream in a bowl and
gives Lizette the electric whisk. Jake Monkey
is sitting on the work top watching Lizette.
Lizette switches the whisk on. But oh dear,
she's not paying attention to what she's doing.
She's not holding the bowl straight and the
cream spatters all over the place. Lizette and
Jake are covered in cream.
Lizette gets a bit of a fright, but Mother just
laughs. They clean the kitchen together, then
sit down at the table to eat a piece of the
freshly baked cake. Without cream.

210

20 November

Knitting a scarf

Elspeth is knitting. Do you know what she's knitting?
It's a scarf. A scarf for the winter. Elspeth has only just started.
First she chose the colour. Brown. Now she is knitting the first
bit of the scarf with two knitting needles. Elspeth doesn't
think knitting is very difficult, but she can't do it very fast.
Luckily there is still some time before winter really begins.
Elspeth will have enough time to finish the scarf. When it is
finished, Elspeth will be nice and warm when she puts it on.
And then she can knit one for Gary Monkey. She'll be able
to do that much more quickly, because Gary is much smaller
than her. Elspeth has decided to knit a blue scarf for Gary.
Won't that look nice?

21 November

The climbing tree

Bart Monkey is still only small. He has only just started monkey school. Monkeys learn a lot at monkey school. They learn how to climb. There is a real climbing tree at the monkey school. Bart is allowed to climb the climbing tree today. He takes hold of a branch very carefully. Then he climbs upwards very slowly. He's a bit frightened. The tree looks so terribly high. Then he climbs a bit higher. Then he decides he wants to go down, but he doesn't dare to. He looks down. Oh dear, he's so very high up. Bart can hardly look. But here comes the teacher. She helps little Bart climb down. What a relief, he thinks, to be back on the ground! He's not frightened any more. It will probably be a bit easier next time. He might even climb right to the top of the tree, just like the big monkeys.

22 November

The kind, old monkey

Somewhere in the wood
lives a monkey old and grey.
He might be ninety-nine years old,
I really couldn't say.

He has a very long, grey beard,
and glasses on his nose.
(The beard is on his chin, of course,
where else would you suppose?)

He is a kind, old monkey.
If you visit him, he'll make
a very special treat for you,
of lemonade and cake!

23 November

In the car

Rocky is going for a drive in the car with Father. He has brought his toy monkey with him. Rocky and his monkey sit in the back seat, and Rocky holds him up to the window so that he can see out.
"Look," says Rocky, "that's where my friend James lives. And that's my school, and that's where the baker lives, and there's the playground."
Father has some shopping to do, so Rocky shows his monkey all the shops.
Rocky would like to go out in the car with Father again tomorrow.

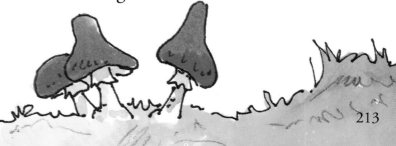

24 November

A bird table

Joseph and Davey Monkey are playing in the wood. They've been busy all day. Joseph and Davey are making a bird table. It will be winter soon and the weather will turn cold. It might even snow. Joseph and Davey like the snow, but the birds don't. If there is snow everywhere, they can't find any food. So this is why Joseph and Davey are making a bird table. They will put food on the bird table for the birds. It will have a roof on it to keep the snow off. They will put nuts and seeds out and perhaps some breadcrumbs, too. So, even if it does snow this winter, the birds will still be able to find something to eat. Isn't it a good idea? I'm sure the birds are happy that Joseph and Davey are making them such a lovely bird table.

25 November

A treasure box

Muriel Monkey has a beautiful box. It is a treasure box. Muriel puts all the special things she wants to keep in this box. There are lots of things in it already. There is a peacock feather and a coloured stone. When Muriel was at the beach, she found lots of pretty shells. The shells are in the box, too.

Muriel has just found a very nice button, a red, yellow, and blue button. She puts it in the box. It's a very good way to keep special things, isn't it?

26 November

The monster monkey

Somewhere in the forest,
a long, long way from here,
in among the tall trees
stands a castle, dark and drear.
The monster monkey lives there.
He is a horrid pest.
He's very mean and likes to steal
bananas from the rest.

Riding a horse

Timmo the circus monkey is bored. There is no performance today, so he has nothing to do. All the animals are at a loose end. Look, there's Bella the horse just wandering about. "Shall we practise some tricks together, Bella?" suggests Timmo. Bella nods her head. Timmo leaps onto her back. Bella trots round in a circle and Timmo pretends that he is bowing to the audience. They're certainly not bored any more.

28 November

The animal ambulance

"Tootaa, tootaa!" Whatever is that noise? Matthew starts and looks around. "Tootaa, tootaa!" There it goes again. An ambulance comes round the corner. Its lights are flashing and its siren is wailing. That is the noise Matthew had heard. "Tootaa, tootaa!" it goes again. Matthew can now see that it is the animal ambulance. Perhaps it has come from the zoo. Do you think one of the monkeys is ill? Perhaps they are taking it to a doctor. It's not very nice for the monkey, but the animal doctor is very clever. He made Matthew's dog better once, so he's sure to be able to cure a sick monkey.

29 November

Hot chocolate milk

It is very windy outside. The trees are leaning over in the wind. Roddy is cycling home. He has to cycle into the wind. He is hunched over the handlebars and breathing heavily. Then it starts to rain. Roddy has forgotten his raincoat, so he gets wet through. When he gets home, Roddy takes off his horrible wet clothes straight away and puts on some dry ones. Then he sits by the fire with his toy monkey. Mother brings him a big mug of hot chocolate milk. Mmm, delicious. He's already forgotten about the wind and the rain.

30 November

Laura, the baby monkey

Look in that cradle.
You'll see tiny Laura.
She's a sweet baby monkey,
don't you adore her?

She has tiny hands,
and tiny wee feet,
a very tiny mouth.
She's so soft and sweet.

This cradle of pink
was made just for her.
Go to sleep, tiny baby,
our darling Laura.

1 December

The snow monkey

Maria is playing outside. It is very cold, but Maria hardly notices. She's far too busy.
Last night, when Maria was asleep, it snowed heavily. When Maria awoke this
morning and looked out of the window, it was as if the whole world was white.
There was snow everywhere … on the rooftops, on the trees, on the grass, and on
the cars. Maria got herself dressed very quickly. She ran straight outside to play.
She wants to make a slide, and a snowman, and lots of other things. She's going
to be busy all day. She's not alone, because there are already lots of children
playing outside.
"We're going to build a snow monkey," shouts Tim. "Are you going to help, Maria?"
They get down to work. The monkey is nearly finished and looks very good, just
like a real monkey with a friendly face. Then Mother calls out: "Maria, time for
breakfast!"
Maria goes inside. All that hard work has made her hungry. But she's going to go
outside again later. She's still got to make a slide!

2 December

Goodbye, snow monkey ...

Maria gets up early again today. She's going to play outside in the snow again.
She wants to build a snow house for the snow monkey they all built yesterday. But
what's happened? When Maria gets outside, she can't see the snow monkey anywhere.
All she can see is a small heap of snow. Mother laughs. "The snow has melted, Maria.
If the weather gets a bit warmer, the snow thaws and melts. You'll just have to wait
until it snows again." Maria sighs. What a to do. You just get something finished,
then you have to start all over again!

3 December

New snow

My snow monkey has disappeared!
My snow monkey has gone!
The sun just keeps on shining.
It's not fair on anyone!

Tomorrow it might snow again,
and make the world all white.
I'll build a brand new snow ape.
It will be a splendid sight!

4 December

Baking cakes

Peter is bored. Not just a bit bored, but very bored indeed. In fact, Peter has been bored all day. Mother told him to find a book and read, or go and play football, or play tag with his friend Rick, but Peter doesn't want to. Peter doesn't want to do anything. Then Mother has an excellent idea. "I know what we'll do," she says. "We'll go shopping first, then we can make some cakes with my new animal shapes." Peter likes this idea. So, an hour later, Peter is busy helping Mother put the cake mixture in the monkey shapes.
He thinks he might make a hundred monkeys!
Do you think they will taste nice?

5 December

Monkey-vision

When Grandpa comes to visit, he always brings a present with him for Margie. Today Grandpa has brought a toy television. Margie can turn the knobs herself to make the pictures of monkeys appear on the screen.
All sorts of monkeys: big ones, small ones, ugly ones, beautiful ones, thin ones, and fat ones!
Margie plays with her television all day. She makes up stories about all the monkeys. She likes this much better than ordinary television. By the end of the day, she is great friends with all her television monkeys.

6 December

Chicken pox

Julian is in bed. He doesn't feel at all well.
There are red spots on his face: Julian has
chicken pox.
"You'll be better soon," says Mother.
"Just you lie back in bed and rest."
"But what's wrong with me?" asks Julian.
"What does chicken pox look like?"
Mother picks up Julian's toy monkey and
a red lipstick. She gives the monkey red
spots all over his face, hands, and feet.
"Look," she says, "your monkey has got
chicken pox, too. You both look the same.
You'd better take him to bed, too, because
now he's got the chicken pox as well!"
Julian and his monkey fall asleep together.
When Julian wakes up, they both
feel quite a bit better.

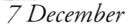

7 December

The tricycle

Paul Monkey has a beautiful bicycle. It is not just an ordinary bicycle. It is a three-wheeler. I bet you can guess why it is called a three-wheeler! Because it has three wheels, of course! One wheel at the front and two at the back. Ordinary bicycles have just two wheels. Paul has had a go on an ordinary bicycle, but it wasn't a great success. He kept falling off. But he's quite happy on the three-wheeler, because you can't really fall off one. He's enjoying himself enormously. He feels he can cycle really well.

8 December

Baghdad monkey

There once was a monkey
who came from the East.
He wanted lots of money
to buy himself a feast
of chocolate and ice-cream,
and sweet things galore.
He couldn't get enough to eat,
he always wanted more!

9 December

The tower of blocks

Yuri is playing with his blocks. There are big blocks and small blocks. Yuri has built a tall tower. It is nearly finished. Just one more block on top. Yuri stands and stretches his arms and legs. He fetches his toy monkey and sits him down next to the tower. "There you are," he says, "now you can see my lovely tower." Yuri puts the last block on the top of the tower. But oh dear … an accident! The whole tower topples down, right on top of his poor monkey. At first Yuri is disappointed, but then he laughs. "Never mind," he says to his monkey, "we'll just have to build a new tower!"

10 December

Hibernating

Outside it is very cold. Everything is frozen. Thomas and Hunky Monkey are out walking in the wood. They have their gloves and scarves on.

"Hey, look," says Hunky, "there's a hole at the bottom of that tree."

"Yes," says Thomas, "I can see it. I bet that's a hedgehog's hole. The hedgehog will be asleep now, because hedgehogs hibernate. It is far too cold for them to be outside in the winter, so they curl themselves up in their warm holes and go to sleep. They only wake up when the weather gets warmer."

Hunky doesn't understand. Who would want to sleep all winter long? Winter is fun! You can go skating and sledging. I'm certainly never going to hibernate, thinks Hunky.

11 December

Funny faces!

Micky and Millie Monkey are bored. "Gosh, I'm so bored!" says Micky, and he rolls his eyes.

This makes Millie laugh. "You do look funny when you do that," she says.

Micky does it again and sticks his tongue out at the same time. Millie laughs even louder. Then she sticks her tongue out and squashes her nose with her finger.

Now it's Micky's turn to laugh. Then Mother comes into the room.

"What are you doing?" she asks.

"We're pulling faces," replies Micky. And he does it again.

Mother laughs. "You pair of funny-face pullers!" she says.

224

12 December

The monkey from
Tyne and Wear

Now listen here, now listen here:
I know a monkey from Tyne and Wear.
His nose is in a funny place,
it's next to his ear, not on his face!

Now listen: what I'm telling you
about this ear is all quite true.
You'll find his nose under his hair.
Just what is a nose doing there?

13 December

The itchy jumper

Grandma has knitted a lovely jumper. It is purple and has a picture of a monkey on the front. The jumper is for Tammy. "Look what I've made for you," says Grandma. "Oh, it's lovely," says Tammy, "is it really for me?" "Yes," says Grandma, "try it on to see if it fits." Tammy tries the jumper on. But oh dear, the jumper itches. Tammy begins to scratch. "Grandma," says Tammy, "I really like the jumper, but it's very itchy." "Is it really?" asks Grandma and feels the jumper. "I see what you mean," she says, "it does itch, doesn't it? Never mind, I'll make you another, just as nice as this one, but one that doesn't itch!" Tammy is delighted. Isn't Grandma kind?

Birthday

When Caro wakes up in the morning, she thinks: today is a special day. Today is my birthday! She runs downstairs. Father and Mother are already up.
"Good morning," they say, "did you sleep well?"
"Yes, thank you," says Caro and sits down at the kitchen table. That's funny, she thinks, why didn't they say anything else? Have they forgotten that today is my birthday? Father is reading the newspaper and Mother is pouring the tea.
"Today is a special day," says Caro, "have you remembered?"
Father looks up from his newspaper. "What do you mean, a special day?"
"It's my birthday!" says Caro.
"Oh dear, what a thing to forget!" says Father.
Then both Father and Mother begin to laugh. They have been teasing Caro. Of course they haven't forgotten her birthday. Father goes and gets her present. Mother brings in the cake to show her. There are five candles on the cake, because today is Caro's fifth birthday. Caro will be allowed to blow out the candles at tea time. Now she may open her present. It is a beautiful toy monkey with a key in it. When you wind it up, the monkey walks all by himself. He turns his head, too. Caro has completely forgotten about the cake. All she can think of is her lovely monkey!

15 December

A squirrel

Ellie and Nellie Monkey are out walking in the wood. Suddenly something whooshes by them on the ground. "What was that?" asks Ellie. She is a little bit startled.
"Oh, I see now," she says. "Look, there, in that tree." She points upwards.
"Oh," says Nellie, "it's a squirrel. He's collecting food. When the snow comes, he won't be able to find anything to eat any more. The snow hides everything. So he's collecting as much as he can now."
"How very clever," says Ellie. "That means when it's really cold, he'll be able to stay in his nice warm hole and he'll always have enough to eat."

16 December

Pyjama monkeys

Hello there, just look at me,
and see what I've got on:
a smart pair of pyjamas
with monkeys marked upon.

Brown and black monkeys,
front, and back, and side.
Among the black and brown
a white one may just hide.

And when I go to bed at night
to have a great big sleep,
I say "Goodnight, pyjama friends,"
as into bed I creep.

227

17 December

Sliding

Chris and Jacob have thought up a good game. It's exciting, too. Chris climbs onto the banister rail at the top of the stairs and slides all the way down. "Now it's your turn, Jacob," he calls out.
Jacob gets onto the banister rail. One, two, three ... swoosh. Jacob slides down just as quickly as Chris. "Wheehee!" cries Jacob, "this is fun! Now it's Monkey's turn."
But Monkey isn't very good at sliding down the banister. He can't hold on properly. He falls off and bumps his way down the stairs. Ouch, he lands on his head!
Chris and Jacob decide that they'll carry on without him.

18 December

A new winter jacket

Terry wants to play outside, but it is very cold. He needs a new winter jacket, because he has grown out of the old one. Mother takes him shopping to buy one. Terry knows straight away which jacket he wants when they get to the shop. The red one with monkeys all over it. It is just his size and is lovely and warm. Mother likes the jacket, too, which is lucky, because she has to pay for it. Tim is allowed to keep it on. Now he can go outside to play. He certainly won't be cold any more.

228

19 December

Gloves on a string

"Mother," calls out Jimmy, "have you seen my gloves anywhere?"

"No," says Mother, "you haven't lost them again, have you?"

"Yes, I have," answers Jimmy.

"I don't know what's got into you," says Mother, "that's the fourth time this week that you've lost a glove. What do you do with them?"

"I don't know," replies Jimmy. "I try to look after them, but …"

"Right," says Mother, "we'll have to think of something to stop you losing them all the time. I've an idea." Mother gets a new pair of gloves and a piece of string. She ties one end of the string to one glove, and the other end to the other glove. Then she puts the gloves down the sleeves of Jimmy's jacket. A glove hangs out of each sleeve. "There you are," says Mother, "now your gloves can't escape from your jacket. You won't be able to lose them any more."

Jimmy is very pleased with his new gloves. Mother promises to embroider little monkeys in blue hats on them. He's never had such lovely gloves, and now he won't lose them either!

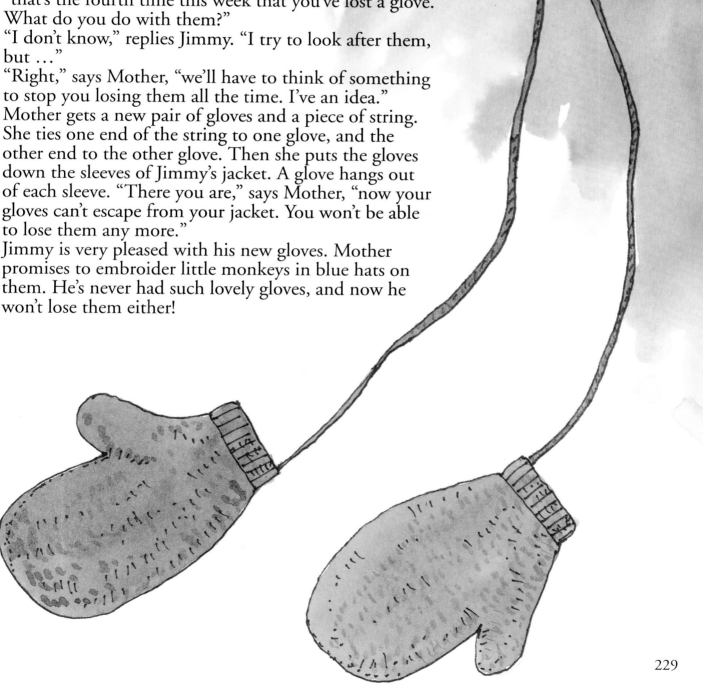

20 December

The forgetful monkey

I know of a monkey
who wears a gold ring.
He's one of those monkeys
who forgets everything.

He forgets his new jacket
and then his left shoe,
and when he goes shopping,
he forgets what to do.

I think it must be catching
(though some may be appalled),
for I seem to have forgotten
just what this monkey's called!

21 December

Winter begins

Today is a special day. It is the first day of winter. In the winter it is very cold. It gets dark very early in the evenings. Sometimes it rains heavily and there are high winds. The monkeys don't much like this sort of weather. But they do like snow. All the wood is then white with snow. The trees, the grass, everything. When there is a lot of snow, the monkeys build snowmen. And they go sledging.
Sometimes it freezes hard in the winter. Then the streams and the lake in the wood turn to ice, so the monkeys can go skating. There are some monkeys who wish it were always winter!

22 December

Making Christmas cards

Yvonne is sitting at the table. She is making her own Christmas cards. She makes a card from a piece of paper, then she draws a picture on it with crayons. Yvonne has already made a card with a Christmas tree on it. And one with a candle. Yvonne wants to make lots of cards, because she wants to send them to all her friends. Grandpa and Grandma must get a card, too. So must all her aunts and uncles. Yvonne draws a picture of a sweet little monkey in the snow on the next card. She likes it so much that she does a few more monkey cards. When she has finished all her cards, she puts them in envelopes, sticks stamps on them, and posts them in the letter-box.
Yvonne has really enjoyed making her Christmas cards. I think she's very good at it, don't you?

23 December

Choosing a Christmas tree

Micky Monkey is out in the wood with his father. "Are we there already?" asks Micky. "Nearly," replies Father, "just a bit further." They reach a part of the wood where there are lots of fir trees. "Look," says Father, "here we are. Now we must find a nice fir tree to take home." "Oh good," says Micky happily. It is nearly Christmas. Every year, at Christmas, Father gets a fir tree from the wood. Then they decorate it at home to make it into a Christmas tree. This year, Micky is allowed to go with Father. "I've found one!" shouts Micky. "No," says Father, "that's far too big. We'd never be able to carry it home." They walk on a bit further. "This is a good little tree," says Father. He chops it down very carefully and ties a rope around its trunk. That way he will be able to drag it home behind him without pricking his hands on the needles. "May I go with you again next year?" asks Micky. "If you're very good," says Father.

24 December

Christmas in the wood

Just look, just look
at our beautiful wood.
The trees are all dressed
for a party, that's good!

The monkeys all gather,
they're full of good cheer.
They're going to celebrate
Christmas this year.

With presents and tinsel
on a tree nice and tall.
"Happy Christmas" they say,
"Happy Christmas to all."

25 December

Decorating the Christmas tree

Millie Monkey is allowed to decorate the Christmas tree with Mother. Millie takes the baubles out of the box very carefully. Then she hangs them in the tree. "Look," she says, "this one is just like a mirror. I can see my reflection in it. Don't I look funny. My nose looks huge!" Then she puts the tinsel round the tree. She has nearly finished. There's just the special decoration left for the very top of the tree. Millie can't quite reach, so Mother does it instead. "There," says Mother, "the Christmas tree is finished. I think it looks beautiful, don't you?"
"Oh yes," says Millie, "absolutely beautiful!"

26 December

A Christmas story

Jon and Christine are sitting by the Christmas tree with Father and Mother. The tree is beautifully decorated with lots of baubles and tinsel. Jon and Christine have just been singing Christmas carols. Now Father is going to tell a Christmas story. Christine sits on Father's knee and Jon sits by his feet on the floor.

"Once upon a time, a very long time ago, there was a tiny fir tree in the wood. This little fir tree wanted very much to be a Christmas tree, but it was far too small. All the other fir trees had been taken away. They were already in people's nice, warm houses, waiting for Christmas. He was all alone in the wood. He was very sad, so sad that he almost cried. But along came a tiny little monkey. This little monkey didn't have a Christmas tree in his house. He wanted a tiny Christmas tree, but he hadn't been able to find one. Here was just what he was looking for! So the little monkey took the tiny fir tree home with him. He decorated it so that it looked quite beautiful. So the tiny fir tree did become a Christmas tree after all!"

"What a nice story," says Christine when Father has finished.

"Yes," says Jon, "it had a very happy ending!"

27 December

Flowers on the window

When Edmund Monkey wakes up in the
morning, everything is frozen. He gets up
and goes over to the window. He tries to look
outside, but he can hardly see anything
through the window. There's something on
it. He touches it. Brrr! That's cold! It looks
like ice. There are pretty patterns in it.
Mother comes into the room. "What is the
matter?" she asks. "Look what's happened
to the window," says Edmund.
"Oh that," says Mother, "those are frost-
flowers. If the window is a bit wet and it
freezes hard, the water turns into ice.
The patterns in the ice look a bit like flowers,
don't you think?" Edmund agrees, but he
thinks it sounds funny.

28 December

Footsteps

It's snowing, it's snowing,
the whole world is white.
"Ooh!" cries Monkey Tom,
"what a beautiful sight!

Everywhere I go,
I make footsteps on the ground,
whether I go left or right,
or round, and round, and round.

Look – you can see them,
footsteps in the snow.
They follow me just everywhere,
and will not let me go!"

29 December

Shovelling snow

It has been snowing in the wood. Everything is covered in a thick layer of snow. Terry Monkey wants to go outside. But he can't get the door open. There is a pile of snow blocking it. Terry looks out of the window. Father is busy shovelling the snow away. Terry quickly climbs out of the window to go and help. "Father, may I help?" he asks. Father gives Terry a small shovel. Together they shovel all the snow away from the door and pile it up in a heap. "There," says Father, "all the snow is out of the way. Now we'll be able to open the door." Terry has already got his sledge. He can't wait to slide down the big pile of snow.

30 December

Sparklers

Mother has given Ellie and Iris something very special: sparklers. They have to put on a glove and hold them carefully right at the bottom of the stick, then Mother will light them. As they burn, they give off pretty, sparkling stars. "I can't see properly," says Ellie. "I'm too close."
Mother picks up Ellie's toy monkey and puts a sparkler in his hand. Then she lights it. Now Ellie can see beautifully. Doesn't it look lovely? "Oh look," she says, "a sparkle landed on Monkey's head!"
Mother laughs. "Never mind," she says, "I don't think Monkey minded, do you?"

31 December

The very last day

Today is the very last day of the year. All the animals in the wood are celebrating. They are celebrating New Year's Eve. That is the day before the new year begins. Everybody, even the very smallest monkey in the wood, may stay up until twelve o'clock. Because, at twelve o'clock precisely, the old year ends and the new year begins.

Millie and Micky Monkey are also having a party. Mother and Grandma have been busy making delicious things to eat all day. Millie likes banana fritters best. Father lights the fireworks at twelve o'clock. There are rockets that shoot up into the sky. First you hear a bang and then they explode into lots of lovely colours: red, white, blue, green, and lots more. They look wonderful. The fireworks mark the end of the old year and the beginning of the new. Everyone wishes each other: "Happy New Year!" After such a big party everyone is tired, especially the little ones, so they all go off to bed. So do Millie and Micky.

Night, night, and sleep tight. See you in the new year!